Saved
by Mr. F. Scott Fitzgerald
and other Stories

Saved

by Mr. F. Scott Fitzgerald

and other stories

Allen Woodman

Livingston Press
The University of West Alabama

ISBN 0-942979-41-9, paper
ISBN 0-942979-42-7, library edition

Library of Congress Cataloguing in Publication #96-78841

Manufactured in the United States of America.

Text and cover layout and design by Joe Taylor
Proofreading by Beth Grant, Lee Holland-Moore, and Stephanie Parnell

***Printed on acid-free paper
first edition***

Portions of this book have appeared, sometimes in slightly different form, in the
following: *The Akros Review, Apalachee Quarterly, Beloit Fiction Journal, Cali-
fornia Quarterly, Carolina Quarterly, The Crescent Review, The Double Dealer
Redux, Epoch, Flash Fiction, Four Minute Fictions: 50 Short Stories from the
North American Review, Mainichi News (Japan), Micro Fiction, Mirabella,
Mississippi Review Web, The North American Review, Outerbridge, Story, Snake
Nation Review, Sudden Fiction (Continued),* and *Swallow's Tale Magazine.*

The author wishes to thank, in Alabama, Dr. Joe Taylor, Helen, and the *real*
George. On the Gulf Coast, thanks to Inez and Sandy. Thanks, elsewhere, to the
following: Bill, Glenn, and Paul; Carlson, Carver, and Brautigan; NAU and the
Arizona Commission on the Arts; Jerry and King; Rick-Dog, Barbara, the Ice-
man, and Ashé.

**Livingston Press specializes in Southern and off-beat literature,
most happily when the two meet.**
For a complete catalogue of our books, write to
Livingston Press
Station 22
The University of West Alabama
Livingston, AL 35470

Table of Contents

for Jane

THE CHRISTIAN VENTRILOQUIST

Even as a child, my lips were rigid. My entire body was very still. I used to sit for hours, not moving, not speaking. My father was embarrassed to bring his friends home for lunch. He called me Dummy. My mother longed for possibilities. She thought my silence bred some kind of genius.

She would take me to the music stores and set me on piano stools and place French horns and clarinets in my hands, but still my fingers did not decorously flex, my mouth remained frozen.

It was when my mother had only one aspirin left in the bottle in the medicine cabinet over the kitchen sink, after my father had long since left over the purchase of expensive art supplies, that her inspiration came. She borrowed a TV from Uncle Hoot. She had him fix an antenna onto a pole for better reception. She set me on a little blue bathroom rug in front of the television all day long. She felt the technology would help. Every few minutes she would stop her housework and walk into the room to see what was showing on the screen and see if the sight of it had changed my posture or expression.

Her wish for shape and purpose in my life turned to despair when my hands did not tremble before the visions of Lawrence Welk or Liberace. But then my throat betrayed me.

During an Edgar Bergen movie, as Bergen made his ventriloquist doll, Charlie McCarthy, talk, my throat began to vibrate. It was a cough or a vowel sound, I've never been quite sure which, but my mother came running, and there I was with my jaw and lips rigid, and my throat making ugly sounds that held for her so much beauty and hope.

Then we were in the car driving to Eastbrook Shopping Center, to Woolworth's, and the Dixie Rexall. Then we were whirling down aisles, my mother's hands disappearing under stacks of Mr. Potato Head sets and Barbie Dream Houses.

The druggist at the Rexall sold my mother a special device from a rack of colorful gimmicks. It was in a plastic pouch right next to the finger-snapper pack of gum and the plastic dog poop.

The paper inside the pouch showed a workman carrying a steamer trunk on his back, startled by a voice coming from inside saying, "Let me out of here." It was a mechanism for "Throwing Your Voice." My mother bought it, and, back in the car, she made me put the small whistle, the sole contents of the pouch, in my mouth.

I could not throw my voice to another place or even speak a word. I could only make the sounds of a high-pitched whistle. My mother threw the disc out the window like a tiny, silver bird.

At Toyland, her search ended. There in the back of the store, next to the model kits of the Knights of the Round Table, was a genuine Charlie McCarthy ventriloquist doll, dressed in his familiar black tuxedo, top hat, and monocle.

At home we found the string that operated his mouth. It came from a tiny hole in the back of his neck.

For the next two weeks, my mother would read the pamphlet that came with the doll to me and help me with the exercises. She would put me in front of her makeup mirror, on her knee, and I would put Charlie McCarthy on my knee. She would help me recite the alphabet, and, when my lips lost their tight control, she would pinch me on the arm with her long red fingernails. We left out six letters: B, F, M, P, V, and W. My mother said the instructions told how we would learn the substitute sounds for these labials and plosives later. She worked at night coming up with words and phrases that didn't use them.

For days the words came with violence or vanished without a trace or sometimes my lips would bend down out of their fixed smile and my breath would heave like a pigeon's breast. And still my mother would hold me and remind my skin of my mouth's imperfect murmurings. Until, one by one, the letters came and then the words and phrases. Until, with each breath, I could faultlessly hiss, "She sells seashells Sunday at the seashore."

She sewed a tuxedo for me that looked just like Charlie McCarthy's. She made a monocle for me out of a broken pair of eyeglasses. She had to buy a top hat at a dance supply store.

Next, we were standing in the Garden Club Room in the back of Flink's City Florist. The women all wore the same dust-colored dresses. Each held in her hand her favorite variety of daffodil. There were trumpet and large-cupped blooms and a sprinkling of doubles and short-cups in cluster types. The flowers ranged in color from deep gold to pure white.

I was billed as Little Ed and Charlie, Jr., and, after a short script my mother had borrowed from an old Shari Lewis TV show, my finale arrived.

My mother had driven to Atlanta and spent almost ten dollars at a magic shop for a trick glass that appeared to make milk vanish. It only took a small amount of liquid to make the glass look full, and an inner chamber caught the liquid when the glass was tilted and spread it out so that it looked as if I were actually drinking the milk. My mouth was freed up behind the glass to form even the toughest of sounds.

As I held the glass to my lips and pretended to drink, I recited a Wordsworth poem, "I wandered lonely as a cloud that floats on high

3

o'er vales and hills...." I made my Adam's apple bob up and down as if I were drinking. "When all at once I saw a crowd, a host of golden daffodils...." And as I continued reciting, the ladies in the group stood up in unison and thrust their prized flowers in the air and began to sway, vigorously absorbed in the landscape of blooms.

"And then my heart with pleasure fills, and dances with the daffodils," I finished. My mother thanked the ladies and added that it was a special pleasure to be there today since it was also my seventh birthday. I had already had my seventh birthday two months before, but just the thought of it brought the ladies marching forward to embrace me against their thick, white necks and still larger chests and press a dollar each into my tiny hand.

For eight years my mother kept me in the public eye with bookings at nursing homes, American Legion posts, and Elks clubs in Mobile, Dothan, Selma, and Montgomery. She developed a fancy anti-smoking script where Charlie Jr. appears to blow out my match every time I tried to light up a cigarette. The PTA loved the idea and we were invited to almost every elementary school in Alabama and Georgia.

When I was fifteen, my mother met a man who owned three doughnut shops in Birmingham. We were the guest act at the grand opening of his fourth store. After the show he took us back to his house for dinner.

Charley Jr. and I sat in the dirty kitchen. I ate from a box of day-old crullers. My mother and the man watched TV in the living room.

My mother kept making this loud laugh. It sounded like a crow. I peeked out the kitchen door. My mother had her dress pulled up. She was sitting on the man's knee. He kept whispering something to her, something he wanted her to say.

I sat back down at the kitchen table. Charlie Jr. sat in the chair next to me. We were still dressed exactly alike in our matching tuxedos, except I had taken my hat and monocle off and left them in the man's car.

I started to eat some chocolate twists, but my eyes kept looking at Charlie Jr. He seemed to keep getting smaller and smaller, or maybe it was just that I felt like I was getting bigger and bigger.

I walked out the back door of the house to get some air. The stars over the trees and houses in the neighborhood seemed so tiny. I kept walking.

Dressed in the black tuxedo, I had no trouble catching rides. Truckers would stop just to rib me about how I must have gotten lost from my senior prom.

I headed south for Gulf Shores. Once, Mom and I had stopped for gas there on our way from Pensacola to Mobile. It was a beautiful little place along the coast of Alabama with the whitest sand I had ever seen. And towering above the sand, just under the bright sky, were golden yellow beach houses stuck up proudly on pylons. I wanted to stand very still in the sand and look out into the green water of the Gulf of Mexico and know that silence was the best language ever spoken, but we were on a schedule and due in two hours at a women's club tea room in Mobile.

I arrived at Gulf Shores at dawn. I walked out beside the Pink Pony Pub and the Sea Horse Motel to where the water met the jagged creosote poles of a decaying fishing pier.

The water moved towards me in graceful ripples that reminded me of the way a magician's silk scarf might flow in front of him just before it changes colors between his huge palms. I did not think about what I would do the rest of the day or the next. I did not think about how odd I would appear dressed in formal wear standing perfectly still in the white sand when the others arrived with their coolers and Hang Ten towels and Frisbees. The beauty of the Gulf carried no overwhelming need of thought.

I stayed on the beach all day, sometimes standing, sometimes sitting, hoping that the sun would fade away the black fabric of my clothes and hoping that the salt would corrode the leather and brass of my shoes, but by evening time all I could feel changed was the exposed skin on my face and hands. As the night closed in, I took my shoes and socks off and dug my toes into the giving sand, unconcerned with what life lay beneath it, the sand crabs and spiders. I looked into the moving water, my eyesight failing, searching for the dark outline of boats moving beyond the sandbar.

I wondered if people out on those boats would be able to see me sitting so motionless on the shore. And then I heard whistling. It was not the metallic sound of my first ventriloquist whistle. It was the sweet human sound of air pressed between lips. At first, I could only see the glint of something silver, something barely the size of a woman's slip showing beneath a hemline. Then, as the figure approached, the silvery form revealed itself as the aluminum leg of a summer lawn chair.

A young woman carrying the chair unfolded it next to me as if I were invisible. She pulled a beer off of a plastic ring that retained two others. She wore a one-piece bathing suit with a sweater tied around her thin waist. Her legs were as white as a pearl against the dark air.

She began whistling again in between sips of beer. The tune meant nothing. Then she stopped and wet her lips with her tongue. I looked down at her feet. Her toes were long and beautiful. I wanted to form some words to say to her. I thought of phrases that would be easy to say. But I feared if I opened my mouth only a stream of air brighter than the aluminum of her chair, whiter than her legs, would come out, arching between us, breaking the perfect silence.

She turned towards me and offered me one of the two remaining cans of beer. Her well-formed mouth invited me with a smile. I took the can and opened the pop-top and watched the beer foam through the small opening. I held the beer up in a kind of a toast. "To the Gulf," I said, "that swallows up everything." Then she tried to speak, but her lovely face twisted and jerked and tried to catch that receding tide of language. Her labor for vowels and consonants told me of her drunkenness.

She could not tie words together to ask of my attire or name. But just her look, past speech, asked me to return with her, carrying the lawn chair back to the only brick cabin on the beach. And there on the bed, under a wooden ceiling fan, she communicated with her breath and tongue against my skin, stopping only to turn the dial of a portable radio that hung from the bedpost by a strap to suitable music.

I awoke to catch the sun at every window. She was lying quietly on top of the sheets.

Then I showered and used a large red beach towel to dry up the water I'd splashed onto the bathroom tile. I looked through her cabinets for some deodorant. I used her toothbrush. I wanted to wake her up with kisses for her eyes and mouth. I wanted to tell her things about why I was on the beach in a tuxedo and ask her about her own night vigil. I wanted to ask her name so I could blow the word sweetly back to her over a generous breakfast of fresh peaches and figs. I wanted to wrap us both in words like soft animal skins. But the telephone rang in the other room.

I opened the bathroom door to see her standing naked, lit in silhouette by the white-lighted window. Her face struggled again to conquer simple words. Her "hello" and "yes" fought their way from her mouth like air from a drowning man's lungs. One side of her mouth pulled tightly while the other side seemed to stretch wide enough to swallow an egg. It brought back the violence of my first struggle, my imperfect words.

It had not been drunkenness the night before but something else.

She hung up the black phone. She wrapped the sheet around her. I dressed and explained that I was going out to look for a job, that I would be back later, but her eyes could see my invention.

She turned and toyed with the radio. It seemed harder to get the right station during the day.

After that, I lived for a while over the Mother of Pearl Dry Cleaners in Mobile. I found a job service that would send me out about three days a week. On the days I didn't work, I just stayed in my room and listened to the steam presses below until I felt too sweaty and stiff to move.

The service had me fill out a list of interests and hobbies, but the jobs never seemed to match them. For several weeks I worked in an icehouse shucking oysters and cleaning crabs, and then I worked a few days emptying trash cans and sorting mail at the newspaper office.

One morning the phone rang. A man from the service asked me to stop by the main office. He called it the *main* office, but I knew they only had one room in a building down on Magnolia Street.

When I arrived the man had my list of interests and hobbies laying in front of him on his desk. He picked it up and fanned his big face with it. He told me how the service prided itself on placing applicants with the right jobs. His lips seemed to move too much for the few words he was saying. It was almost like his words were dubbed.

He smiled and asked me if I wanted coffee. He said the job would last for at least six weeks. He chewed a bit on the end of his pen. He wanted to make sure that I planned to stay in town on the job. There would be a bonus at the end if I did. He gave me the address card.

It was the largest church in Mobile. The banner out front read "Summer Christian Youth Festival." The Reverend took me down a long hall to my classroom. Along the way, he informed me of words and subjects he didn't want me to use in front of the children. He took great delight in going through his mental list as if he had recited it over to himself many times before in private. He also told me he'd be happy to go over the routines and dialogue that I planned to use later for the final Christian Youth Recital.

In the room, I was surrounded by children, all between the ages of six and eight. In each of their laps they held the innocent dummies. The dummies were all fashioned after religious models. Most of the boys had small fiberglass figures of Jesus sitting on their knees, and the girls had been given Virgin Mary dolls. On the instructor's desk in front of the room were other costumed forms of angels, wise men, and even a special baby Jesus in a basket. It was my first class in Christian Ventriloquism.

I slipped my hand inside the baby Jesus figure and found the metal levers that controlled his eyes, mouth, and head movements. The inside of the dummy felt hard like a seashell empty of its soft mollusk.

As I cradled the basket in my lap, I told the boys and girls how to find the control levers in the back of their dummies. They practiced manipulating them.

The cow-eyes of the dummies winked. The heads turned. One of the girls had a more expensive figure than the rest. She could get her Mary doll to wiggle her ears. All of the children wanted to trade with her.

The children laughed and laughed. Then it was time to give them voice. I told them how to hold their jaws rigid. I taught them how to smile and keep their teeth slightly parted. I had them all repeat the simplest of sounds, the sounds made without the use of lips.

I looked around the room and saw the children smiling and heard their droning noises seemingly coming from the sacred figures swaying on their knees. "Ay," I said. They mimicked the sound through clinched lips and teeth. "EE," I cried. Again, they repeated it. "EYE...OH...YOU."

Then phrases returned from my youth, "She sells seashells Sunday by the seashore." The skin on their small faces tightened and strained as I forced them to form harder and still harder sounds and phrases, faster and faster, and in louder voices. "Satan sells seashells Sunday by the seashore."

Their mouths became ugly machines, twisting up and transforming air into sound into life for their faithful dummies. Their struggling faces reminded me of the woman on the beach. Their gasping for the consummate voice, her gasping, my gasping. "Kum Ba Yah," my baby Jesus shouted for them to sing. "Kum Ba Yah," it shouted and shouted. And the girl with the fancy Virgin Mary began to cry and one of the others ran out of the room, trampling over his fallen figure of Jesus as he ran to get the Reverend back, and my lungs felt like they were going to explode and send my heart pounding into the engulfing past.

I'd scare you if I told you any more. I'll only say that after the service let me go, I tried to call my mother. Every time she answered the phone, I couldn't speak. It was too painful. All I could do was listen. She kept shouting, "Speak up! Speak up!"

I thought of going back to the woman on the beach, but I knew it would never work with two dummies. There was only one alternative left.

I'd once read about how in the sixth century before Christ there was a temple built in a place called Delphi. Sometimes the priests there would stand very still and listen for strained sounds to come out of their stomachs. Words would form, but their lips would not move. Then one of the priests would try to interpret the belly-noise for someone who had come to them seeking the advice of the gods. But one day all of the oracles fell silent.

And now, sitting in my small room over the dry cleaners, I wait for their return because I know that memory and loss are just mirrors and time itself comes back like a reflection. And circumspect, I will wait for that tiny private voice within to articulate all possible things, and I will generously listen so quietly and so still that I will hardly be here at all.

WALLET

Tired of losing his wallet to pickpockets, my father, at seventy, makes a phony one. He stuffs the phony wallet with expired food coupons and losing Florida lottery tickets and a worn slip from a fortune cookie that reads, "Life is the same old story told over and over."

In a full-length mirror, he tries the wallet in the back pocket of his pants. It hangs out fat with desire. "All oyster," he says to me, "no pearl."

We drive to the mall where he says he lost the last one. I am the wheelman, left behind in the car, while my father cases a department store.

Once my father took me with him to buy his funeral plan. The funeral director said that the plan included a prepaid burial suit. My father made him throw in an extra pair of pants because he had never bought a suit with less than two pairs of pants in his life. "Just throw them in the casket with me," he shouted. "I want to be ready."

I say it, "I want to be ready," over and over, as I sit in the front seat of my father's Dodge Dart, my fingers gripping and then regripping the leather steering-wheel cover.

In the store, my father is an old man trying to act feeble and child-like, and he overdoes it like stage makeup on a community-theater actor. He has even brought a walking stick for special effect. Packages of stretch socks clumsily slip from his fingers. He bends over farther than he has bent in years to retrieve them, allowing the false billfold to rise like a dark wish and be grappled by the passing shadow of a hand.

Then the unexpected happens. The thief is chased by an attentive salesclerk. Others join in. The thief subdued, the clerk holds up the reclaimed item. "Your wallet, sir. Your wallet." As she begins opening it, searching for identification, my father runs toward an exit. The worthless articles float to the floor.

Now my father is in the car, shouting for me to drive away. There will be time enough for silence and rest. We are both stupid with smiles and he is shouting, "Drive fast, drive fast."

IN THE HALL OF THE LOST WORLD

Cloetta came at the talking weight scale slowly. She circled it as best her two-hundred-and-five-pound, large-boned frame and her small apartment bathroom would allow. She did not want to hear it bark those same admonitions it always bellowed when her huge feet touched its cold black surface.

She had piled her clothes up outside the door and entered the room head down, too embarrassed or disgusted to look up into the mirror that hovered over the white porcelain sink. She thought for a moment about how her toes, barely visible below her heavy stomach, looked like pink grapes about to burst. She almost wanted to touch their juicy knobbiness, but her girth and the prolonged mechanical moans from the encumbered machine prevented her. "Jesus, that smarts!" it professed like the Burning Bush for dieters. "I give! Keep those sodden hips at a safe distance, you clumsy, culinary cow," it spewed. "I'm suffocating. Call the paramedics." And so it continued its plague of crabstick sockdolagers until she was forced to plod heavily out of the bathroom, tripping over her pile of ample garments, all fitted with resilient elastic, past her aluminum Christmas tree, and into the soothing womb of the Sears Kenmore refrigerator.

The mouthy automaton was a gift from little Buckshot. When Buckshot stood on the talking scale in the Big Dixie department store, it simply told him his meager weight in pounds and always added, "Have a nice day." A bored salesperson had changed the internal message tape while Buckshot waited for gift wrapping.

Buckshot was heavy with love for Cloetta, and Cloetta felt that she must return his love. After all, Dr. Buck, Buckshot's father, was Cloetta's employer. But sometimes Cloetta felt that being in love was too much like riding an exercise bicycle.

Dr. Buck, who founded Dr. Buck's Museum of Medicine and the Dinosaur, had told her that even though his son was only nineteen and she was forty-six, it would be unwise, even unsafe, to stunt his son's first expressions of love. Dr. Buck went on to say that if fulfilled, his son's budding clarity of passion would prevent him from becoming a rotting stump of aged emotions. Cloetta would have laughed at Dr. Buck's prognosis but for the fact that Dr. Buck gave her a raise and moved her from the giftshop where she sold Dinosaur T-shirts, scarfs, tattoos, neckties, shot glasses, and bed sheets to the Hall of the Lost World.

The Hall of the Lost World was a large room with eight fiber-glass, plaster, and chickenwire models of savage dinosaurs frozen in a heroic battle for supremacy. Cloetta's new job was to push the four switches that controlled the sound-and-light show that started every half hour. The fierce dinosaur noises blasting from the loudspeakers and the flashing red lights produced the ultimate in what Dr. Buck called the Info-Tainment Factor. He wanted the Museum of Medicine and the Dinosaur to be both intellectually stimulating and entertaining.

The medicine part of the museum contained jars filled with all the organs, tumors, and cysts that Dr. Buck had removed from patients before he retired from surgery at fifty and founded the collection. Many of the growths took on unusual shapes much like those found in popular caves. Dr. Buck had one that was in the shape of a large chapel, another in the shape of a cake, still another was a wedding couple. These were all preserved and placed in one well-lit case under a sign that read *Love Will Out*. Every year, professors from the University of South Alabama Medical School would bring their first-year students on a field trip to see the remarkable specimens.

Next to the *Love Will Out* exhibit was a case of preserved chicken bones and other objects that some of Dr. Buck's patients had choked on. Young mothers liked to use this display as a moral lesson for their children not to gulp their food.

The most popular exhibit had been the larger-than-life visible man and woman. They were both anatomically correct and covered in clear plastic so visitors could marvel at the four-color inner workings of the human body.

There was a control box in front of each figure and buttons to push so that various systems and organs would light up and short taped messages from Dr. Buck would reveal the beautiful mysteries of the mortal form. But school children would often alternately push the male and female reproductive system buttons so that the penis and vagina flashed at each other too closely for the local Parent-Teacher Association. It forcefully encouraged Dr. Buck to sell the visible woman statue to a sister museum in Nebraska.

Cloetta's head had been inside the freezer long enough to cool off sufficiently; she wouldn't throw the talking weight scales out the window. The refrigerated surroundings also helped her to remember the fish dish she was to bring to the Museum of Medicine and the Dinosaur Christmas party. All twelve employees were responsible for bringing something from the sea, and Dr. Buck provided the rest of the feast. Dr. Buck enjoyed the idea of the Twelve Fish Dishes of Christmas. It had a beautiful epicurean symmetry. There were twelve disciples. Jesus was a fisherman. It kept him from ever hiring more or

16

less than twelve employees, even though many of them only worked a few hours each week. He also preferred to hire mostly Catholics because of their family fish recipes, handed down from generation to generation, some inventive enough to make fish appear and taste like veal or pork.

Cloetta decided to make a shrimp mold out of condensed tomato soup, cream cheese, and gelatin. She placed layers of shrimp in a form shaped like a giant crayfish. Then she put the mold up to chill until set. She returned the washed head of lettuce that would form the bed for the mold to the refrigerator too. But something about seeing the vegetable and fruit drawer at the bottom of the refrigerator unearthed her hatred for Dr. Buck and little Buckshot. It came in cold waves. Her hatred for Dr. Buck and little Buckshot was larger than the hate she had for the talking weight scale that Buckshot had given her as a Christmas present, her hatred for them was larger than Christmas itself.

For the past few weeks, every evening, Cloetta would go over to Dr. Buck's double-wide mobile home that sat up on blocks behind the museum and eat dinner with Dr. Buck and little Buckshot. Dr. Buck would always talk during the usual meal of vegetarian-vegetable soup and cheese toast about how television was killing the business at the museum. How all the kids wanted to do was watch TV at home or play video games while they were on vacation. How an educational exhibit like the Museum of Medicine and the Dinosaur had to suffer in a screen-oriented society.

"All history is a giant spectacle," he habitually repeated, "served up to us on the screen daily. War, death, disease—nothing is a mystery. Yet, everything is so direct, so immediate, that it seems fictitious." He would always go on like that, punctuating his position with his sandwich held aloft, until he retired to his room to read *USA Today* and left Cloetta and little Buckshot to watch whatever videotape Buckshot had selected at the rental store.

For several nights Buckshot had selected the same movie staring Susan Sarandon and Burt Lancaster. It was called *Atlantic City*. And he would replay this scene where Susan Sarandon stands over her kitchen sink and rubs the bare skin of her breasts with the flesh of a lemon, hoping to take the smell of her fishy job at an Atlantic City oyster bar out of her pores, and Burt Lancaster would just watch her through the window across the way, and Buckshot would just watch the screen and then smile at Cloetta, and Cloetta would wonder when he'd be old enough to outgrow the little pink pimples that covered his thin face and his spare body. Naked he looked to her like a relief map for a country that boasts numerous foothills or, even, the volcanic landscape of the dinosaurs. She was often afraid that if she squeezed him too hard the pustules would all break in unison and half decrease his modest body weight.

The night before, after seeing that lemon-rubbing scene for about the tenth time, Buckshot got up from the couch, his bumpy skin and the vinyl producing a kind of kissing sound as their suctioned embrace separated.

Buckshot lifted up a large watermelon from behind the kitchen counter. He split it and brought a substantial piece of it hoisted over his head like a jungle prize back to the couch, back to Cloetta's huge belly and jutting breasts that almost formed one perfect parallel monument to women's sexual organs. And Cloetta thought about how another man had once told her that there was something erotically potent about the fact that she always looked heavy with pregnancy, as Buckshot rubbed the juicy section of the melon across Cloetta's luscious form.

18

Then her thoughts were on the terrible lizards in the Hall of the Lost World and how Dr. Buck had once answered a patron's question about how dinosaurs did *it* with the reply that the question was still unresolved. There was no fossil evidence of huge penis bones. And she remembered overhearing a school kid's response to the old saw about where do dinosaurs sit. Anywhere they like. And now she knew that with their huge fangs and claws, dinosaurs did it anywhere and anyway they liked. And she looked upon Buckshot, eyes shut, mouth open with asthmatic breath, and his small, spent frame glued by the primitive sauce of love and fruit sugar to her form.

Cloetta knew there had to be some kind of container for her hate. She imagined her hate sitting up on top of her head like the tomato soup mold of a crayfish, cold and motionless, like something out of a horror movie, keeping her from sleeping or enjoying her favorite TV programs and only allowing her the small concession of eating to block out the terror of it all.

She searched her tiny apartment like a shark of hope, hunting for the thing that would transform her life. She stayed clear of the bathroom where the damnable weight scales waited to mock her and pull her down to the irredeemable depths. And she thought about how living is just the process of weathering hate. And she fell as prostrate as her belly would allow, face down in despair, in front of her aluminum Christmas tree, just inches away from the color-wheel that turned and cast first a red, then a yellow, then a blue, and, finally, a green aura of glory upon her countenance.

The counterfeit tree did not defraud nature by its silver aspect. In contrast, Cloetta thought, it exalted nature.

Cloetta slowly rose and savored in her mind the plan she now understood for ridding herself of her odious feelings. She walked to the kitchen drawer where she stored the back issues of the Museum of Medicine and the Dinosaur newsletter. She found a Xeroxed photograph of Dr. Buck, then one of little Buckshot, and, finally, one of herself.

She took three round ornaments from the tree, and, with scissors and glue, she managed to paste the cropped images onto the glittering balls.

She hung the two ornaments embellished with Dr. Buck's and Buckshot's images up near the top of the lustrous branches. She stood back and gazed at the aluminum Christmas tree that over thirty-five years before had caused her to weep the sweet tears of childhood until her mother bought it at the neighbor's yard sale, her mother not really wanting to use the same tree the neighbors had used before it became fashionable to purchase a fresh-cut, fully flocked one every December. This same artificial tree had now become her Tree of Hate.

Cloetta stood, almost transfixed, holding her own ornate likeness dangling from a tiny hook. She watched the tree hold up the two things she thought she hated the most. There were many more colorful balls on the tree. Plenty of room for other hates. Room for even small dislikes and petty annoyances. And she thought about the frail, thin shell of the glass bulbs, filled with nothing but trapped air.

She had broken enough of them every year to know it. Sometimes they would just fall off the tree and shatter on the floor when no one was around. She would be at work and come home to find one broken on the floor, under the shining branches, and she would look at it with the same kind of wonder and almost sadness she held for the delicate pieces of bird eggshells she would find under the pine trees behind the museum.

It was getting close to the time for the Christmas party. Cloetta knew she would have to check the gelatin mold soon and find a dress to iron and wear. She took the ball that bore her picture and placed it at the very top of the tree in the spot usually reserved for an angel, but celestial ideas were far from her mind. She knew that the Tree of Hate could only hold her real hate, if that, and all others would just fall away.

The Christmas party at the Museum of Medicine and the Dinosaur began, as usual, with Dr. Buck's personal tour of the establishment. He would relate various anecdotal glimpses behind his numerous acquisitions. It was always sort of a beautiful sight to see Dr. Buck in the middle of it all like a man surrounded by a large city he had founded. But when he stood in front of the *Love Will Out* display, encircled by many other tumors, growths, and organs, his voice grew tight. "The language of agony is hard to talk about," he began, and everyone just stopped and looked at him.

Normally, Dr. Buck would just tell some funny tale about a nurse or another doctor fainting at the sight of blood, or how some other surgeon cut up the wrong patient, but this was a different story. Dr. Buck cleared his throat and repeated what he had said, "The language of agony is hard to talk about." He pointed at the lighted case. "I built this museum as a way of rejecting pain. Whenever I operated on a patient, I searched for something wondrous, not just an ugly deformation of the everyday. I wanted to take something out that would let me know that there was still some sort of mystery. And then I wanted to show others that there was some way to rise above the intolerable ache." They were all just silent, huddled together.

"My wife, Buckshot's mother, married me just as I was about to retire from surgery. She was a good bit younger. She kept hoping that I would drop my silly notion of a museum and buy a beautiful house at the beach with window latches and cabinets designed by respected artists. But our dreams never quite meshed." Dr. Buck looked into the case at the organic wedding couple. "But she left me with a son, little Buckshot, and for that she has given my life more grace than she will ever know." Dr. Buck held up an official-looking piece of paper. "And for that, almost twenty years since it began, I am turning over the museum to my son."

Everyone began clapping and Buckshot walked up next to his dad and hugged him. Buckshot spoke up then and said that even if he did begin to manage the place, the museum would always belong to his father. And when someone asked him his plans, he said he only had three things he wanted to change.

The first was to take a truck the very next day and pick up the larger-than-life visible woman up in Nebraska and reunite her with her partner, the visible man. Dr. Buck's eyes welled up with joyous tears as Buckshot explained that times had changed and no one minded hearing about the reproductive systems anymore.

Buckshot's second plan was to expand the museum to include a Garden of the Dinosaur, out back behind the museum, where young people could spend romantic evenings strolling among the illuminated representations of Stegosaurus, Triceratops, and Tyrannosaurus rex.

On his third vision, Buckshot stopped a moment and looked directly at Cloetta. "My third dream," he said, "is to marry Cloetta and bring her home to live here at the museum." Everyone began clapping again and shouting. Someone joked how it would be a good way for the museum to save on salaries.

Cloetta staggered backwards into the unlit Hall of the Lost World.

22

In the black room she could barely make out the shapes of the giant statues. Dinosaurs had ruled the earth for over 100 million years, she thought. Most of them had brains the size of peas. And as Dr. Buck told it, the males may not have even had penises. And none of them ever stopped their lizardly lives to stand on a little black pedestal and find out if they had gained a few hundred pounds.

She also kept thinking here was a boy, under twenty, who wanted to marry a fat, forty-six year old woman. She kept thinking that it just wouldn't last. It'd be like Dr. Buck's marriage, only in reverse. Buckshot would leave or get so bitter that she just couldn't stand it.

She heard Buckshot's voice calling to her, somewhere in the darkened room, somewhere among the giant dinosaurs. "Cloetta, where are you?" And again, "Cloetta, I love you."

Cloetta thought about the Christmas tree back home, the Tree of Hate. She thought that when she got home those balls covered with their likenesses might not even be left on the tree. They might have already come crashing down to the floor. She thought she might even start a tree of the things she loved. It would be another way of surviving. And, if they were still whole, maybe she would just leave Dr. Buck's and little Buckshot's pictures up there on the tree.

Then she imagined how special, even romantic, it would be for Buckshot and her to be driving back from Nebraska on their honeymoon in a pick-up truck towing a giant visible woman behind them. And, suddenly, standing in the dark, she thought about the dinosaurs again and how ruling over the earth for over 100 million years, nearly fifteen times longer than any of her ancestors had existed, wasn't so bad for a bunch of big, dumb pea-brains without any known organs for copulation. And maybe nothing lasted, but love, and love will out.

The Further Adventures Of The Household Saint

You wake one morning to find you can open jars easily. You become obsessed by the ecstasy of turning the metal lids of glass tunnels until their capping surfaces slip away.

You start out small, opening just one jar of Aunt Nellie's Fancy Sweet Peas for your husband's dinner without using the rubber Mighty Grip tool that Claire, the woman at the Valley National Bank drive-thru window, gave you. Your hand becomes the largest part of you. The same hand that usually performs some mundane ritual like fixing the part in your hair becomes one huge appendage moving back and forth against the seeming sureness of the seal, almost tasting its shape and texture, until it breaks and the lid rises like a chalice from a fairy-tale lake.

After you have finished opening the sixth jar of very young, tender peas without the security of resorting to running hot water from the faucet or tapping them with a piece of stainless, you are aware that somehow you have acquired an intuitive knowledge of the secret physics of jar lids, the intricate language of the soft, transparent membrane that holds the present modesty from the future wealth.

Like a domestic archaeologist you explore the kitchen cabinets searching for the one jar that doesn't yield before your newfound talent. You think for a moment of your husband and imagine how glad he will be that he didn't convert to some form of survivalism and buy up a year's supply of provisions stored in airtight jars.

24

All about the room lie bottles and jars separated from their false coverings like open graves on Judgment Day. The sweet foodstuffs rise from their tombs to meet the decay of air. Your cat watches you fill the icebox with jars whose colorful labels read "Refrigerate After Opening."

You move on to your mother's house. You do not ring the bell. You use the extra key she had made for you after she had read the newspaper article about the woman who died locked up in her double-wide with her hungry poodle.

Once inside, you see your mother through the sliding glass door, standing in the backyard. She is bending over. She has a stick in her hand. It looks like she is writing something in the dirt.

The jar of Imported S&W Stuffed Manzanilla Olives With Minced Pimentos has been waiting under the bar since your father fell off the boat three years ago. Your mother had been taking him to Lourdes to bathe in the healing waters. Somehow the way he tripped over a deck chair on the ship and was irretrievably lost in the middle of the Atlantic was strangely comforting to your mother. He had exchanged the concession of soaking in a spring for the full luscious sea.

From time to time visiting relatives would try to open the gold cap of the S&W jar without success. It is the real test. You stare down at your hands. They are clenching and unclenching as if they have no choice.

The jar is not forgiving. It is like trying to put your hands in the pockets of a new suit coat and finding the pockets still sewn shut.

The map of lines on your right hand forms a new territory. You understand that all things in your life have slipped away like the surfaces of the lids. Lately, your husband has given you clues. He does not like the way you fold the towels. At night, after you have gone to bed, you hear him in the bathroom refolding and replacing them in neat stacks under the sink. He has also started humming under his breath a song whose chorus pertains to the fact that sometimes you fail to put a new roll of Charmin bathroom tissue back on the paper roller when the old roll runs out. You opt to leave the new paper sitting upright on top of the toilet tank.

Now the hand surrounding the gold ring of a lid swells to the size of a catcher's mitt. The jar of olives wishes to remain uncompromised, but your fingers cling to their greed. Your arms unbearably ache with the desire to extend beyond definitions.

You hear your mother's voice from the yard. She is calling out some unrecognizable gospel. You leave the opened jar on top of the bar next to the miniature copy of Manneken-Pis, Brussels' seventeenth-century statue of a little boy making water. Your father always exhibited his irreverent spirit when he showed each new visitor how the little man squirted his oily liquid.

Later, your mother will find the exposed jar and read the message in its dark green contents.

At home you call your husband at work. You do not mention your newfound power. He will find out soon enough at dinner when he sits before the mountain of peas covered with pats of yellow margarine, reading in them the history of the day's events.

On the phone you ask him to stop by the supermarket and buy a gallon of skimmed milk. You secretly wish the milk was not packaged in a plastic jug with a pull-off ring for easy access. You are wise enough not to go to the grocery store alone. The aisles of unopened containers would glow too invitingly. You would lovingly stand before the blue caps of the Mott's Clamato Juice bottles, feeling gently with your fingers to make sure the safety buttons on the lids protecting the original seals had not popped up yet.

In the bathroom, you undress in front of the full-length mirror. Flecks of foodstuffs from your many trials cover your clothes, and some particles have even found their way down your blouse and congregate on the surface of your small breasts. You look like a child allowed to feed herself for the first time. For a moment, you are kind to yourself. You do not look in the glass and notice the weight you tend to gain in your stomach area. You choose not to stare at the rough skin of your feet and your yellowing toenails, even though your mother has forever told you that this is where you notice the signs of aging first.

What you do see is your black cat expectantly lying against the cool white porcelain bathtub. He always waits in the tub for you to turn on the water. And when you do, he touches it with his paw. But he cannot catch the translucent rope of water that continuously streams down from the faucet. His paw passes through it countless times, and still he remains focused on the sweet task until the impossibility of it makes you weep with the joy and the understanding that nothing holds and all surfaces slip away.

KISS

I married a woman who was a lipstick model for a cosmetics company. Their ads proclaimed their products were cruelty free and that they didn't test them on animals. We had passionate sex every night, sex so wonderful that I forgot there were stars. The only problem was she would not let me kiss her. She did not test their products on animals either.

We kissed once in Las Vegas. We had both been drinking champagne. It was in one of those wedding chapels across from the Circus Circus casino that look like the perfect Norman Rockwell view of a church, only shrunk down to miniature size so it could easily fit between two huge casinos. It had a big pointy steeple, an arched front door and plenty of stained-glass windows. It was called the Little Wedding Chapel to the Stars, and, inside, the Minister to the Stars had couples waiting in line.

After we checked off the items we wanted from a menu that included various souvenir photos, floral bouquets, selected musical stylings, choice of religious or secular service, and option of long-grain rice or bird seed (the ecological preference), we reverently passed through the Wedding Photo Gallery to the Stars. There were pictures of their famous clients on the walls, forming a perfect gallery of B film and canceled-after-one-season TV actors. Puffy faces, red eyes, toupees askew, the booze and the city seemed to have gotten to them all.

After the cowboy and cowgirl clad couple ahead of us had said their "Yep, I do's" and finished up with a ceremonial roping of the wedding couple by a hired hand *comme* Will Rogers (costumes and roper as featured on the services menu), it was our turn.

We were casually dressed in shorts and matching Caesar's Palace T-Shirts. We had opted for a simple secular ceremony, no expensive extras. But the Minister to the Stars converted our alcohol-induced frivolity to sobriety and focused our attention on what we were doing.

With real conviction he said, "And if you ever think you are not being loved enough, try loving more. Giving love will bring back love." Maybe it was the booze or the heat or the moment, but we both started crying and then we kissed.

The kiss was fast. She winced. I thought of those prostitutes you see on daytime TV talk shows. The ones who say they'll do anything but kiss their clients. One said that "kissing was just too personal."

My wife perfected the Hollywood kiss. You know, the one where it looks like two people on the screen are kissing each other tight with a hot passion, but if you were close enough you could see one person's cold fingers sequestered like a maiden aunt between the two pressing mouths. Whenever there was a moment in front of relatives or friends that called for a familial smooch between spouses, up would shoot two of her fingers faster than a harsh word.

It reminded me of something I read about a photographer who had to take pictures at a nudist colony. There she was surrounded by handsome, naked, young men. But there was one naked man who was wearing a bandage on his ankle. After a while, it got so the only thing the photographer wanted to look at was what was under that small strip of material. That's the way kissing became for me. I had sex. Plenty of it. But what I wanted to remember was which was best: the moment you first take your lips away after a kiss or the moment before your lips are joined tight like butterfly wings?

We tried lots of substitutes. Once she cupped her hand into the shape of a puppet's mouth, licked the side of her hand wet, and tried kissing my mouth with it. She said it was the way small girls first learn to kiss by practicing on their own hands. "Kissy, kissy," she said, but it reminded me too much of Señor Wences on *The Ed Sullivan Show,* too much like kissing a ventriloquist's dummy.

I thought of my history of kisses, of all of the kisses I'd ever been given. Forehead kisses from my mom and kisses on hurt knees, air kisses of aunts, the kiss of peace from perfumed ladies at church, and the kiss of life we practiced in PE class, pressing our lips to a mannequin. I thought of fainting in front of my wife, but she always carried one of those plastic resuscitation masks in her purse. I recalled a girl named Alice in elementary school kissing my eyelids like the smallest brush of a painter's kit. I thought of the funniest place to be kissed and the best place to be kissed. I thought of blowing kisses, of the kiss-off, and the kiss of death. I remembered finding the imprint of a kiss once on a menu in a restaurant: was the red stamp self love or the loneliness of kissing shadows?

I did not think of the later kisses that were just the prelude to taking off clothes. I realized that I had not lingered long enough on the kisses of my youth. The first kiss, the wings of her mouth opening, ruffling against my own, both ready to fly away in a moment's notice. I wondered why teens had to be the keepers of the kiss.

The dictionary says that the verb "kiss" means to touch or press with the lips slightly pursed in a token of affection, greeting, or reverence. And yes, I wanted to touch and press, to smack, peck, buss, graze, caress, brush, and, yes, even to osculate. I thought of that business-minded acronym for KISS, keep it simple, stupid, but that's what I longed for, the perfect, stupid, simplicity of a kiss.

I entered a crowded movie theater as an escape from the kisslessness of things, just minutes after the movie started. I sat down in the dark, before my eyes had yet to adjust, before I realized that the stranger sitting next to me had turned, my hands full of salty popcorn and sweet cola, and grabbed me and placed a full kiss on my mouth. Whether man or woman, mistaken identity or stolen kiss, I rose up like a shout and ran, spilling my refreshments, all the way out the exit door.

Only outside, after slowing down to breathe in the light, did the seed of memory grow. I thought of the long way some people go to arrive at a kiss. Of Snow White's Prince Charming who finds a dead girl in a glass coffin, surrounded by dwarfs, and the only thing he feels compelled to do is kiss her. And how I could find a cemetery for kissing, too, through sleep.

That night, I watched my wife in her sleep. She always slept on her back, one arm behind her head, almost posed for a photo of Sleeping Beauty. I thought it would be easy. I hoped to cover her mouth with a kiss so perfect that she could remember it when she waked. She would recall it like a dream of expectation and wish to act upon it.

But my desire was too ferocious. I knew that my kiss would press too hard or wet or loud with life's worries. So I faltered over her sleeping form, and I thought backwards from climaxes to foreplays to kisses and, before even that, to the moment of desire to kiss, to the moment I was so happy just to see her, that first day, at Starbucks, in line beside me, ordering a *Frappuccino*, the exact same thing I ordered, and her smile when her hand bumped into mine as we both reached simultaneously for the white-chocolate sprinkles.

Then, I burst into tears. And she woke and asked, "Why are you crying?" And I said, "It's nothing, go back to sleep." And I looked down at her, in the dark, strands of her hair misplaced, her eyes half-opened, and her rich mouth filled with the weight of sleep. "It's nothing," I whispered again. "It's only happiness." And she reached up and pulled my face down to meet hers, and we kissed.

WAITING FOR THE BROKEN HORSE

There always remained the doing of things.

Nathan put on his hat. It was an unfashionable felt hat that occasionally he chose to wear. "I'm going out for coffee," he said to Ann, his wife. "Do you have the keys?"

Ann held her face away from his. She was looking at a slick circular that advertised magazines at 50% off and touted a chance to win a vacation home at the beach. They had already retired to a vacation home at the beach.

She decided to subscribe to a magazine called *Farm Wife News*, even though she had never lived on a farm, even though she couldn't think of any future different from her past.

Nathan waited for the silence to break. Silence was part of their relationship.

Nathan dug around again in his pockets. He found the keys. "I've got them," he said.

Once he caught her in an unguarded moment. She was looking in the bathroom mirror. Her mouth was making an occasion out of it. Her lips were the color of ripe red peppers. The color was important to him because he was always afraid of going blind. She was practicing an exercise she had read about in one of her magazines. Her mouth was exaggerating the shape of vowels. It was a positive act, attempting to postpone the haggard skin of long years.

And for a moment he wished that he could place his head down next to hers and mime the gestures that her face was making. And, as if by magic, their faces would laugh together in a kind of toast to the way things can be put back together after they have quietly fallen apart.

At the coffee shop, he ordered the Bottomless Cup. The waitress did not make any other suggestions. The price of coffee did not carry any overwhelming need for exchanged remarks.

He looked into the cup and tried to read its dark contents. He set the coffee back down on the table to cool. He wished that there had been a newspaper in the box out front. The Thursday paper sold according to the cents-off food coupons.

The couple at the table next to him had ordered the Barnyard Bonanza Buffet. It was $3.95 and carried the slogan "all-you-care-to-eat."

Nathan found the system in their numerous trips to the food bar. Their first plates were loaded with protein. The man's plate carried an equal number of bacon strips and sausage links, twelve pieces in all. The woman started to select the links, but changed her mind in midair, and picked up several sausage patties with a pair of silver tongs. Between their plates, Nathan estimated a scrambled egg count of nine eggs. It was enough to empty any small farmyard of life.

Their next plates were for the carbohydrates: hotcakes, French toast, and biscuits, all covered in cane syrup; grits and butter, and hash-brown potatoes and ketchup. And these were followed closely by the fruits-of-the-season plates laden with orange slices and melon plugs.

As the couple were asking the waitress whether the soup of the day came with the Barnyard Bonanza, Nathan looked outside the window. He was a little embarrassed that he didn't have anything better to do than to see how much food people could eat. It kind of reminded Nathan of something a radio-preacher had said once over the airwaves

34

late at night about fast days. "Yes," he said, "keep them when there's neither bread nor bacon in the cupboard."

In the vacant lot next to the coffee shop, a young man had posted a sign that read *Merry-Go-Round Rides $1.00*. It was not the brightly painted and ornamented apparatus of the circus that played every year beside the state fair. It was reduced to bare bones, to wooden poles without a touch of paint. And the sculpted wooden horses were replaced by one broken nag pulled along by a frayed rope.

Nathan gave up his right to the Bottomless Cup of coffee. He walked over to the lot. He longed for something beautiful.

There was no music. The wood creaked as it turned in a tight circle. With a stick and shouts the young man drove a grey horse. The horse's once-smooth coat was sliced by the plain shape of bones.

Nathan watched a boy that seemed far too heavy jumping up, now and again, upon the horse's sloped back. The horse moved stiffly around the ring in an absent-minded way.

Nathan looked at the multiplicity of half-ring shapes that the animal's hoofs had made in the sand.

"Care for a turn?" the young man asked.

Nathan was startled. "That horse," he said, "looks like it's ready for the pasture."

"Just a pure waste of space. It wasn't even worth shooting when I got it."

"It looks like it's starving," Nathan continued.

"It's just *lean*. You know, *a horse is a horse, of course, of course....*"

Nathan didn't understand the man. He had never watched *Mister Ed* on television. He had never seen any talking-horse shows. But once he had seen a movie about Francis, The Talking Mule, who managed to cause a great deal of trouble for his innocent sidekick, Donald O'Connor. What Nathan did next he understood even less.

"Why not sell it and get a *real* horse?" Nathan asked.

The man swatted the horse's back with the stick. He felt that special feeling of value for an unwanted item that someone else covets.

Nathan offered the man three hundred dollars for the horse. It was a high price, but Nathan had never bought a horse before. In fact, Nathan hadn't bought much of anything in years outside of a few irreclaimable items picked up at garage sales.

Nathan went home and waited in his backyard for the man to deliver the horse. It was a small yard, even by beach house standards. Nathan had never been one to want to putter around in a garden or trim shrubs to look like things other than shrubs.

Inside, the house had dwindled to a single room where his wife sat stacking and restacking magazines. She thought about buying an Early American magazine rack to go beside the couch.

Outside, Nathan imagined her discovering the horse. She would stand beside it. She wouldn't say a word. There comes a point where there's no more virtue in words. Then her hand would brush the fuzzy hairs that radiated about the horse's eyes. She would not know why she did this. She would feel the hot flushing of her face, and strain to say, "Good boy." And without touching, it would be like Nathan and his wife were holding hands.

"It won't be long," thought Nathan, as he waited in the yard.

VINYL REPAIR

Noble was absently sprinkling salt over half a ripe tomato when he saw something black lying in the sand next to the shoreline. He had been re-coloring the vinyl seats in the High Tide Motel lobby from blue to red, and was now taking a few minutes for lunch. It was off-season and no one was in a hurry.

The black spot turned out to be an abandoned bikini top. Noble examined it. It had a label that read, "Cole of California, Size 36B." It pleased Noble to look at it. He hadn't expected such an item.

Noble thought about the act of a woman in white-hot summer pulling her top off and smoothing her skin with smears of cream or lotion. It was easy for him to love the things of people he didn't know.

Once he had a job repairing the mayor's chair. Some kids had broken into his office and burned holes on the arms of his desk chair with cigarettes. The chair was only brown naugahyde, but it had once belonged to the mayor's father. Noble fixed the arms and re-conditioned the whole chair so well that when the mayor sat down in it and rubbed his hands across the places where the damage had been he started to cry. Noble followed suit in a friendly, unreasoned way. It was like he had loved that old chair, too. Neither of the men was known for easy tears.

Noble held each cup of the top in his palms and imagined the breasts that once filled them. Then he replaced it on the sand where he had found it. Noble walked back to the lobby and started re-coloring the seats. Colleen came out from behind the front desk to watch. He was going to tell her about the bikini top, but he didn't. He thought it'd be like telling a secret someone had made him promise not to tell.

"That red color's good. It's what the lobby needed," Colleen said.

Noble placed his brush into the Perma-Bond Color Coat can. "This'll color anything," he said, and pointed to his white shoes. "Guess how old my shoes are?"

"They look brand-new," she said.

"Three years old. I coated them myself a week ago."

Colleen brought out a pair of white shoes from her kitchenette in the back. "Can you make these new again?" she asked.

"Wherever I see vinyl, I can do business," he said, and traced his fingers along the shoes' outlines.

"They were my wedding shoes," Colleen said. "My Warren loved me so much that he tried to kill me with them. He threw me around this very lobby one night. I kept banging into those chair legs. Then he pulled the shoes off my feet and started hitting me on the head with them. He kept shouting parts of the wedding vows, 'To have and to hold. Till death do you part.'"

"What happened?"

"Since then, I've never been able to go to another wedding. I can't even stand to watch one on TV."

"No, I mean about your husband?"

"He shot himself in room seventeen. A guest heard the shot and told me. When I opened the door, I didn't even recognize him. I thought it was some tourist."

Noble waited to speak. He could feel she had more words to get out.

"If the Tastee-Freez hadn't been closed he would still be alive. Every time we had a fight he'd go next door and have a chocolate

38

malted. Sometimes he'd bring me back a cup of soft-serve. But this time the Tastee-Freez closed early. There was a closed sign on the door. The boy inside cleaning up remembered my husband coming by and banging on the glass."

Noble didn't know what to say. They were just standing there looking at each other, and looking at the shoes.

"I'll restore these free for you. But tell your friends I charged you three dollars," Noble said.

She offered him a cup of coffee. She had just made a fresh pot.

Noble sat down on the sofa in Colleen's room. The sofa was perfect. No holes or cracks in the vinyl. Colleen gave him some coffee and sat down beside him.

"Doesn't sound much like love," Noble said.

"It was love."

"The way he beat you with your wedding shoes?"

"It was true," Colleen insisted.

Noble lifted his coffee mug in salute. The mug had an illustration of a card from a Monopoly game. It was Boardwalk. Monopoly was Noble's favorite board game as a child. He wondered if his childhood edition was still around, stored in an attic someplace. It was nice to think about that game for a few seconds. He remembered giving it up about the same time he stopped reading the Sunday comics. "Then love is knowing what to overlook," he finally said.

Then he did something. He didn't know what else to do. He picked up her hand. He felt the hard bones under her skin. What good bones, he thought.

Afterwards they sat up on the sofa. Their knees bumped. "Now say something so I don't feel like a whore," Colleen said.

Noble took her hand again and raised it to his lips. He was thinking about the tan lines that made cuts where her torso had been separated from the sun. She looked like some sort of board for a game that had not been created yet. The sections of unsunned flesh seemed luminous.

"We're lucky," he said, and thought about how the vinyl coating he would use on her shoes would be sturdy and how it would last longer than anything else.

BONES OF MARRIAGE

Inside Harley's head was a mule skull. It was the skull that kept her from balancing her checkbook. She tried keeping checking accounts at two different banks, and every month she would alternate using them, but still the mule skull compelled her checks to bounce. She even devised a new system where she recorded one dollar more than the real amount of purchase for every check she entered in her check register, but still she would go over her balance. And the skull didn't just interfere in financial matters. It was the skull that allowed the breakfast dishes to pile up and totter in the sink like aged acrobats. And, in general, it was the skull that made Harley's heart feel as flimsy as a failed Frederick's of Hollywood honeymoon negligee.

Harley started noticing the effects of the mule skull over a year back when her husband first discussed the idea of using dishwater detergent to wash her long dark hair. Harley was buttering a slice of bread when he started reading an article to her from one of his many consumer information magazines. The article told how even the cheapest brand of dishwashing detergent would wash your hair as well as any fancy brand of hair shampoo. It was the kind of item Harley did not want to hear. Harley did not want to give up her Fabergé Organics shampoo with pure wheat-germ oil and honey. She was already tired of having him nag her for not washing out the plastic wrap and reusing it after it had covered the spaghetti leftovers for a week.

After their talk there was a small insistent sadness to the breakfast toast each morning. And whenever Harley walked in front of a mirror she could see that old mule skull shining through. Somehow it reminded her of the fluoroscope machine the Eastbrook shoestore used to use to show patrons that their new shoes were big enough. When the store wasn't busy, the salesman would let Harley just stand in front of the machine and slip her bare feet into the bottom slots. Then, through the view port at the top, she could watch the bones of her toes wiggle.

Back when Harley was in the fifth grade, she had collected an entire mule skeleton at her grandfather's cotton farm. Her grandfather had taken her out into the field and shown her where the buzzards and ants had precisely picked the bones of tissue and meat, leaving only the white contours behind. Harley knew the larger bones would be perfect for show-and-tell.

Show-and-tell took place in the fifteen minutes before the last bell of the day rang. Mrs. La Farge, Harley's teacher, called her to the front of the room, but when Harley pulled the mule skull from the bag, Mrs. La Farge found that they didn't have enough time left to see all of the bones Harley had brought. Harley was disappointed that she wasn't allowed to assemble the complete skeleton on the wooden floor in front of the class.

Harley assured her mother that there was no need for her to pick her up after school. Harley was sure she would be able to carry the burlap bag filled with mule bones the five blocks home by herself. But on the way, the bones grew heavy. She tried to take a short cut across a neighbor's backyard. The burlap sack got tangled in the wire fence. Harley left some of the spilled bones lying on the neighbor's lawn.

The feeling the neighbors must have felt when they first spotted the strange whiteness of the bones lying in their yard was how Harley felt now, twenty-four years later. The bones of her marriage were all about her.

It was a hotter August than usual, and Harley was out driving her small car, hoping that the heat might make the mule skull desert her head for cooler quarters. The windows of her car were rolled up. There was no air conditioner. Her husband decided that she really didn't need one in her car since she didn't have to wear suits every day the way he did. He worked at the leading Pontiac dealership in Alabama. He had to keep up his professional image.

Harley checked the rear view mirror, praying to see the foreign bones leap from her forehead like spring bass jumping for grub worms. Harley made sure her visor was pushed up so that the sun could not miss her face. Finally the glare made her look away from the windshield for a moment, and then she saw them.

They were dogs on the roof of a house. There were at least five of them, two-stories in the air. One of them was a white German shepherd, and there was a tiny silver poodle. The others were mixed breeds. It made Harley forget about her husband for a moment. She no longer thought about how the mule skull made her head feel heavy.

The dogs all seemed to be staring at her in an almost mythic way. It was as if the dogs had stepped out of a fairy tale and were living wondrously in the time frame that surrounded Harley's life.

Below these dogs on the second story roof, Harley felt small. There was no language invented yet that had a word for how unimportant Harley felt before this immensity of dogs.

Harley did not know how long she sat in her car in front of the house thinking about those beautiful dogs until her eyes filled with tears. There was no way of knowing how long the woman in the front yard of the house waited watching Harley watching her dogs until the woman came up to Harley's car window and asked if she was all right.

It was then that Harley noticed the driveway of the house filled with objects. There were soccer balls, bows and arrows, tennis rackets, a popcorn popper, and a super-8 projector and screen. It was the ordinary spectacle of failed possessions.

Harley got out of her car and started looking at the woman's wares.

"I put those dogs up there to keep them from tearing down my curtains inside." The woman was trying to explain to Harley about the dogs. "I don't have a fence around the yard, and I can't let them go around sniffing and barking at my customers."

Harley smiled at the woman. She did not need an explanation for the dogs. The dogs looked silently down at her.

Harley was looking at a 3-In-1 table. "That's a beauty, isn't it?" the woman said, and then began demonstrating it to Harley. "It converts from a pool table, to a poker table, to a formal dining table."

The woman showed Harley the poker side. It had a brown vinyl surface, and there were recessed beverage holders and chip trays. The woman also drew Harley's attention to the pedestal leg. It only came on the deluxe edition.

"I bought this table for my Nick," the woman continued. "He was always going out to play cards or pool. I thought this would help keep us together." The woman showed Harley how the pool table reversed to a dining table. "That's a solid-color walnut tone on that laminated plastic surface," the woman pointed out. "Anyway, when Nick came home and found out I had spent over six-hundred dollars of my savings on this at JC Penney, he poured himself a stiff drink and said that he went out to play pool and cards to get away from me."

The woman's words felt like quicksand to Harley. She felt the smooth green bedcloth of the bumper pool surface. The white, rubber-covered bumpers reminded Harley of the bones she had left in that neighbor's yard.

The woman started telling Harley about how the table made her think of an episode she had once seen of *The Beverly Hillbillies* where Jed, Granny, Jethro, and Elly May were all sitting around a pool table eating possum in what they thought was a fancy dining room. But Harley didn't really hear her. She was looking up at the dogs, then past them to the sky that looked like a giant blue knife against the roof of the house. It was the same sky over Harley's house, except Harley's house was only one-story high.

Harley had always wanted to live in a two-story house, but her husband picked out the house they now lived in. When Harley suggested a two-story house, he said that when they were old they would have trouble climbing the stairs.

The telephone started to ring inside the woman's two-story house. The dogs on the roof started barking. It was like a dog chorus of sorts, and the roof became the dogs' choir loft.

The woman asked Harley into her kitchen. The phone rang fourteen times before the woman answered it. Harley had read in *Miss Manners* that it was proper for a caller to wait between six and eight rings before hanging up.

"Who is this?" Harley heard the woman say on the phone.

Harley noticed the pile of unopened bills stacked on the kitchen table. She knew the look of long-overdue notices. The envelopes were thinner than ordinary bills. Sometimes they came disguised as telegrams.

Harley knew the feeling of not wanting to open bills, too. Harley would stuff the unopened envelopes into her recipe drawer. The telephone and cable bills would lie down beside a recipe card for tuna-stuffed tomatoes.

The woman on the phone sounded angry. "I don't care what my husband told you. You don't know a thing about our situation. If he's lonely without me, then I'm the Queen of England."

The woman was on the phone for ten minutes. Harley didn't know what to do. She tried to remember if she had ever seen a picture of the Queen of England. She wondered how much the woman on the phone resembled the Queen of England. She had gotten all of the English royalty confused in her mind. She started picturing the Queen Mother, who was much too old to be the woman on the phone.

Finally, the woman hung up on the caller.

The woman offered Harley a cup of tea. It was a small consolation for her patience. The woman searched the cabinets for some Earl Grey she thought she had. "It's so much better than ordinary tea," the woman said. And, in the moments of her search for the tea, Harley could almost imagine that the woman was the Queen of England, whose servants had been given the day off so that she could recapture some form of earlier innocence in making the tea herself.

The woman did not brew the tea in a pot. The Earl Grey tea was already in tiny bags that the woman dropped into two mugs filled with hot water. Harley's mug had an illustration of a dog holding a cat by its tail and dipping it into a mug like a tea bag. Harley turned the mug to the other side. Harley could feel the blood moving in her hands. The other side of the mug was illustrated with a cat dipping a mouse into a mug like a tea bag. The mouse's tail dangled like a string from the cat's teeth. All of the animals had the happiest expressions on their faces as if they were just giving each other a nice, warm bath.

Harley assumed that the woman's mug would have an illustration continuing this animal dunking cycle. Harley wondered what the mouse would find to dip like a tea bag into a mug, but the woman's mug didn't have a picture. It just had a message that read, "You're ugly and your mother dresses you funny."

"Thank God for tea," the woman said, and held up her mug in salute. Harley and the woman laughed like she had just told the funniest joke in the history of funny jokes.

The woman told Harley how her husband had gone off the wagon and took her savings and bought a condominium down in Key West. Every once in a while he would meet a woman at a bar and tell her how lonely he was and tell her how his wife wouldn't move to Key West with him. Over the past year the story had taken on new twists with the man adding a part about how he had been told by his doctor to move to Key West or else he would die. And the woman from the bar would invariably call up to give his wife trouble for not moving with her husband. The woman told Harley how once in a while she could hear her husband in the background egging the woman on and probably grabbing at her dress.

The woman explained to Harley that it did not make her feel bad that her husband had never asked her to go with him in the first place and had never really wanted her to move to Key West, but what made her feel terrible was the thought that another woman would betray her with a call.

In the driveway, Harley picked out a croquet set and a food dehydrator. Harley didn't really need them, but she bought them with the same feeling a woman on a diet might employ when buying a chocolate cake at a church bazaar.

Before Harley left, the woman pointed up to the roof where the dogs were lying, silently eyeing them. "Sure I can't pack one of those up for you?" Harley and the woman laughed together again.

Harley promised to come back and visit the woman. Harley knew, though, after a few weeks she would not even remember which house she had gone to. She would only remember the haunted look the dogs had given her.

On the way home, Harley stopped by the Winn Dixie grocery store. In the parking lot, there was a Goodwill pick-up box. The box was shaped like a dollhouse. On the front of the collection box was a drawer like that of a mailbox. Harley was able to fit the croquet-set pieces into the box, one by one, but the food dehydrator was too large to fit. Harley left it on the ground in front of the small structure. She did not want to have to explain the purchase of the items to her husband.

In the grocery store, Harley asked the meat department manager for the largest bones he had. The manager brought out several bones. "These will make a fine soup," he said.

Harley examined them. None of the bones measured in size beyond the scale of her hand. Harley asked him if he had any larger, more generous bones.

The meat department manager laughed and said, "Just these bones I'm standing on." The meat department manager was a very funny man. Harley would often see him holding up one of the chickens from the meat-counter case, waving it through the air and telling some shopper a new meat department joke. And, afterwards, Harley would notice the way the same customer would move about the store straining under the weight of delight.

Harley took the bones from him. She walked past the lamb, the New York strip steaks, and the fish fillets. At the front of the store, Harley watched her soup bones ride along a tiny conveyer belt towards the check-out clerk.

The meat department manager had tidily wrapped the bones in plastic and attached a pricing label, but when the woman tried to make the electric eye read the bar code on the label, the machine wouldn't pick up the price.

The clerk angrily picked up the package of bones as if it had been just another head of lettuce. She rang up the purchase of bones manually.

At home, Harley was washing the breakfast dishes when her husband arrived.

He had had a hard day trying to sell Pontiacs. Everyone wanted to buy a Honda or a Toyota. He had even seen the superior service rating of the Japanese cars in his consumer information magazines.

He poured himself an iced drink. He came into the kitchen and put his arms around Harley as she used a Dobie pad to scrape away the remains of uneaten food off the pans and plates.

He thought she was taking a renewed interest in cleaning up the house. She was smiling. He thought she was in a good mood for a change.

He moved in closer and started kissing the tiny hairs at the back of her neck. He did not see how her eyes looked out over the sink through the kitchen window to the white bones lying on the back lawn.

THE CRUELTY OF CHAIRS

The chairs waited in the Trout brothers' converted basement workshop. They had waited such a long time that they had forgotten what they had remembered of the forest. They had become horrible. They dreamed of breaking old men's backs.

Harry Trout waited in the basement as well. Harry made the exquisite hand-turned legs and frames, and Dave, his younger brother, fashioned the delicate cane bottoms. Together they erected chairs that were wondrous to behold. But wonderwork was out of fashion, and sales were few.

Harry's face was gentle and distant. He was not thinking about the chairs or the pains of old men's backs, even though he was an old man. What he was doing was dreaming backwards of a woman who lived in another time. He dreamed of caressing Sarah Bernhardt's leg.

It was an article in the "That's Entertainment" section of the local newspaper that had started Harry's reverie. The paper was small enough that a section on amusements and the obituary column were on the same page. The article told how Dr. Denuce amputated Sarah's afflicted right leg, almost to the hip, on February 15, 1915, and how P.T. Barnum offered her ten thousand dollars to display the severed leg in his exhibition. After her convalescence in a pine-surrounded villa overlooking the tranquil Bay of Arcachon, the doctor tried to fit her with a wooden leg that was attached by a heavy girdle that clung about her hips and stomach. But Sarah hated the idea of ever wearing any sort of corset. She flew into a rage and ordered the thing thrown into the fire.

Sarah's solution was to have a litter chair specially designed with two horizontal supports by which she could be borne about. It was finished in Louis XV style, painted white and ornamented with gilt carvings. And when she was carried about she assumed the attitude of an empress in a ritual procession. Her arms full of roses. Her wild hair crowned with a capote of flowers. Her mutilated figure a mass of velvets.

Dave, the cane-weaving brother, finished eating a bowl of Raisin Bran and drinking the last beer in the house. He smiled a moment thinking to himself how Harry had earlier picked the raisins out of his own toast so that Dave could have extra fruit with his cereal. Dave wished the telephone would ring. He had gotten bored with reading the "Comics" section that Harry had left for him on the kitchen table. He wanted another beer, but Harry would only let him have one a day. It was not that Dave was a heavy drinker, but he was weak in the head. People had said so often enough for him to hear, and he had to remain clearheaded for the caning.

If the phone rang, he would answer as Harry had taught him to do, "Trout Brothers' Chairs. Chairs the Three Bears would love." Actually, Harry had taught him to say that many years before. Now, Harry would just as soon Dave answered the phone with a simple "Hello" or "Trout Brothers' Chairs."

Ten more minutes passed as Dave waited for the phone to ring. He picked the receiver up, stared at it, and practiced answering. The telephone was the silent black kind.

Dave climbed down the steps into the basement and stood by Harry.

Harry's eyes were closed. His mouth moved like he was eating a chocolate bar. Then his eyes opened slowly to see Dave staring at him.

"Did you like your cereal?" Harry asked.

Dave nodded his head. "Yes, Harry. What you been doing down here?" Dave didn't want to tell Harry that every time he found him asleep, he was afraid that Harry was really dead, gone, and had left him behind.

Harry read Dave the article about Sarah Bernhardt's leg.

"How awful," Dave cried. "So what did she end up doing with her leg?"

"I don't know," Harry answered. "She probably had it cremated with the wooden one."

"Sarah Bernhardt," Dave said, letting the name float in the air with nothing to follow, as if he were repeating a name someone had given him over the phone.

Later that afternoon, the Trout brothers got into their Ford pickup and drove in silence to visit Otto at the home.

Otto Maddox was a war buddy of Harry's. Otto had even been decorated for heroism. But when Otto returned from the war and found out that his wife had made a career move from beautician to poodle groomer, well, Otto gritted his teeth. Fighting overseas so his wife could blue-tint a retired housewife's hair seemed ethical enough, but the very thought that he had killed so that his wife could paint poodle toenails changed Otto.

"Jeez," was all he said. Then he picked up one of the client's toy poodles by the hind legs, held it carefully away from him, and swung the dog like a baseball bat. The dog's head kept connecting with his wife's head. Their yelping merged. The dog was small, but tough, and so was the wife.

Flora, his wife, and Sassha, the poodle, weren't injured but the pet's owner never returned Sassha to Flora's. Flora had photographs made showing the bruises on her neck and shoulders. She had Otto placed in a special home.

The home had a colonial facade with a row of rocking chairs chained to the porch. Dave rubbed his hand over the seat of one of the rockers. He wondered if the owners of the home thought they needed the chains to keep the chairs from sneaking away in the night. "This is where Otto lives," Dave said to nobody.

The Trout brothers were surprised that Otto was not in his room. The windows were wide open. A cleaning woman was going over the room. The TV set that was usually playing *Hogan's Heroes* about this time was dead quiet.

For a moment Harry thought they had entered the wrong room. The floor was wet. Everything smelled of Lysol and soap. Then he noticed the medal-clad uniforms still hanging in the wardrobe.

The cleaning woman straightened up. "He's been moved to the freight room. They need this room for a new patient. It's a shame he died. He was the only war hero we ever had, but I can't for the life of me remember which war he was in."

Harry sent Dave to wait out front. Then he stopped in the restroom to wipe his face with some cool water. In the mirror, he saw the reflected row of black-seated toilets and the dried bits of excrement and urine stains beside every commode. There was no need to curse the old people. They were weak and taking strong medicine. It happened before they could sit down.

Harry tried to open the door to the freight room. It was locked. He felt like kicking it in, but he knew his foot couldn't budge the steel deadbolt.

He found the cleaning woman in the auditorium. She was tearing down and storing two-hundred white chairs. The white chairs wanted to stay put. They wanted to be covered with dust. Harry helped her with them. He even started humming, thinking about the patients two-stepping on the cleared floor that night. And he imagined Sarah Bernhardt's leg in the center of them all, hopping and kicking and dancing unencumbered.

Outside, Dave thought Harry was going to say something, but he didn't. Dave knew what had happened.

Harry sat down in one of the plain rockers beside Dave. He started to rock, but the chain kept holding the chair back. Dave looked at Harry's eyes.

Dave reached over and squeezed his brother's hand for a minute. When he let go of it, he felt strange, like somehow he was suddenly made Harry's older brother.

Dave looked at the rocking chair he was sitting in. He wondered how it would look painted white and ornamented in gilt carvings. He patted its armrest. He motioned for Harry to get in the truck. In his mind he was already breaking the chains.

ᘔHE ᔕILENCE ᓍF ᘔEXTILES

It was not the kind of thing one would normally think about upon rising. But Irene thought, "Someone is going to buy bed linens today."

She stared for a moment at her own sheets. She could hardly escape them. The design was modest, but the material had a high thread count. She had purchased them at a discount from Nan, a fellow sales associate at Burdike's. The manager had been at the dentist's office having a wisdom tooth extracted. The manager would not have approved of the discount because Irene had already used her home fashions discount coupon for a set of raspberry colored towels made of one-hundred percent Pima cotton.

Irene had not asked for the reduction. Nan had simply written the sheets up and put them in a bag. The store had a policy that employees could not write up their own purchases. It was only after Irene had arrived home, after she had placed the sheets on the bed and ran her hand across the coolness of their still surface, that she noticed a twenty-percent discount had been applied to the sales receipt.

The sheets lost dignity.

Irene had saved a small amount each week out of her paycheck to purchase the sheets at full price. She had formed the idea on paper.

Irene had made a chart like a giant thermometer. Its singular purpose was to graph the increments of savings towards the goal of new bed linens.

She had written the combined price of one fitted sheet, one flat sheet, and two standard pillowcases across the top of the chart. The total came to eighty-two dollars. The price did not include matching comforter, dust-ruffle, sham, breakfast pillow, or neckroll. Irene colored in her progress on the chart with a red magic marker. She had seen the same method employed on a public TV phonathon.

At the kitchen table, Irene stopped thinking about her bed linens. She smelled something dead. It was a different way to be awakened.

Rather than the rolling contours of sheets like miniature hills, the smell of something dead formed a larger landscape.

Irene put down her butter knife. She put down the slice of Pepperidge Farm date-walnut bread. She stood up and looked behind the white refrigerator.

She had wanted an avocado colored refrigerator, but she only rented. She told her friends it was coconut-white.

She moved the refrigerator a few inches from the wall. She was looking for something she didn't want to find.

There was no mouse. There was only a small box of bait. On the side of the yellow poison box was an illustration of a dead mouse lying on its back crossed over by a big red X.

The bait was untouched, but just knowing it was there brought the smell of death to Irene's mind.

Beside the bait box, there was a small piece of paper about the size of a fortune cookie fortune. Irene picked up the slip of paper. It was the inspection slip from her new bed linens. It read, "Inspected by Number Five."

The tiny piece of paper made it possible for Irene not to smell the aroma of death. She wondered about Inspector Number Five.

56

As Irene made up her bed and placed the pillows perfectly against the headboard, she imagined Inspector Number Five gently checking on the quality of her sheets as they hurtled forth out of the huge sewing machines. He would hold them for a brief moment and touch them to his firm chin or soft cheek. His beautiful eyes would be able to tell even the smallest imperfections in the fabric. He would be good-looking by even her father's standards. Her father was a truck driver. He thought that every man should look like Clint Eastwood, even a linen inspector.

Before Irene left her apartment for work, she touched a delicate amount of perfume to her wrists and throat. It was a sample of Obsession. The sales associate at the fragrance counter had given the tiny bottle to Irene on her twenty-second birthday. The smell of Obsession was at the other end of the scale from the smell of death.

Irene saw Nan standing by the home fashions station when she arrived at work. The store did not have cash registers. Each department had a station desk and each sales associate had a cash drawer. The sales receipts were all written out by hand. In *Burdike's Guide for New Sales Associates*, Irene had read that Donald Burdike had decided against cash registers so that his customers would realize that individual needs were more important than profits at Burdike's. But Nan told Irene that Burdike had just stolen the idea from Lord & Taylor. Irene had also learned in the *Guide* to never ask, "May I help you?" It counseled to ask more leading questions such as, "May I show you something new?"

Irene could never tell the color of Nan's eyes because they were always just barely open. "Too much TV," Nan said to Irene.

"Selling sheets can be exhausting, too," Irene responded, but she really didn't mean it. Selling sheets kept Irene aware that she was still breathing, and it helped her forget the bad year at Palm Beach Junior College.

"We've got a new memo from Mr. Burdike." Nan handed the note to Irene. "It's Donald's new slogan for the week."

"Be your own decorator," Irene read aloud. "Achieve individuality in your home in keeping with your own tastes."

"New sheets in from Japan, too." Nan held up one of the sheets. It was covered with tropical flowers and parrots.

"It looks like a Hawaiian print."

Nan held up another sheet as Irene refolded the first. "Alligators. This one's covered in tiny alligators. Do they have alligators in Japan?"

"I think they have a special year for them," Irene said trying to imagine the Japanese word for alligator.

"I don't remember seeing any alligators on *Shogun,*" Nan said.

"You saw *Shogun,* too?" Irene asked.

"*Hai,*" Nan said. It was the only Japanese word Nan could remember from the show. "Means yes. I've seen every movie that Richard Chamberlain has ever made. I even bought a copy of the book, but without Richard Chamberlain playing Blackthorne right there in front of you on the screen it's hardly worth it."

Irene thought about how her father wouldn't like Richard Chamberlain.

Most of the day Irene stared across the store towards the escalator. Irene liked to think that people who ascended to the home fashions department on the second floor were special and they somehow cared a little more about their homes and things in general. And Irene took special pride in the fact that their first view of the second floor was of the towel wall.

The towel wall held all of the new towels in the latest colors. This year the towel colors were all named after fruits. Last year they had been named after minerals.

Irene and Nan were responsible for making sure there were no spaces in the towel wall. And they had to make sure that all of the towels were folded in exactly the right way so that their dobby borders formed a perfect vertical line from ceiling to floor.

Late in the afternoon, a man got off of the escalator. He was old. He was not the kind of man who caused much interest in sales associates.

He headed straight to the linens. He looked closely at all of the sheets. He bent down next to them like a sighted person in a blind man's dream.

He rubbed his hands together. He pulled at the skin under his chin. He made soft clicking noises with his tongue against his teeth. No one in the store was aware that even at the man's advanced age, it was the sound of a tongue clicking against original teeth.

He stood over the same patterned sheets that Irene had recently purchased. He stared at them. He was intent. Then he turned around and walked past the sheets. He toyed about in the towel section. He looked at the towel wall, but his vision kept returning to the sheets.

Back and forth he moved in a little textile ballet.

The man's behavior disturbed Irene. She cared about selling sheets. Nan decided to take a coffee break.

"May I show you something new?" Irene asked the man when she caught him again standing by the linens.

"No. Thank you," he said. He did not look at Irene. His vision rested on the sheets. He rubbed his hands together.

"You can be your own home decorator with these linens. They make wonderful curtains, too."

"Yes, they are good sheets."

"Two-hundred thread count."

"Some of the finest," he said. He pulled at his chin. His mouth moved. He made a clicking sound again.

Irene smiled. "Let me know if I can help you find a special color."

"Thanks," he said.

Irene moved back to her station. The old man walked back and forth. His mouth was moving. He was pulling at his chin. It looked like he was talking to his hands.

Nan returned from her break. She made tiny circles with her finger in the air. Her finger spiralled closer and closer towards her head like a rocket on one of those late night TV movies spiralling towards a fiery crash into a planet known only as the letter X. It was Nan's signal to Irene that he was an insane shopper. Oftentimes, people would escape from retirement homes and come back to department stores looking for china or linen patterns that hadn't been made for fifty years.

Irene again asked the man if he was looking for something special.

"Those are good sheets." He started to smile.

"What size is your bed?"

"Doesn't matter. I was just hoping. . . ." The man rubbed his hands together. "See, I could have been a truck driver."

"My father is a truck driver," Irene said. "We have several patterns available for waterbeds."

"Not long hauls. Just short. Sand. I'd deliver it to folks' beach houses. I'd wear those leather driving gloves."

60

Irene remembered that the *Guide* suggested showing a special interest in the customer's needs. "Would you like to sit down a moment?" she asked.

"No. I sit all day." He pulled at his chin. "I was hoping to get to see someone buy a set of these sheets." He held up a flat sheet. "See, I'm on vacation."

"Oh," Irene said. "People buy them every day. I can guarantee that they're comfortable. I have some myself." Irene wished that she could tell the man that the sheets were made of actual linen or at least one-hundred percent cotton, but they were only fifty percent cotton.

"Then your sleep is my cemetery," the man said.

"Sir?"

The man's mouth moved. He rubbed his hand across his mouth as if he were catching the words.

"Irene didn't know what to say. "We have free monogramming this week on those particular sheets," she finally said.

"I thought that was just for towels?"

"No, sir. It gives the customer that special pride of personal identification." Irene was almost quoting directly from the <u>Guide</u>.

The man picked up another flat sheet. Then he put it back. Irene was glad that he didn't open the package. Most customers tore open the plastic wrapping around the sheets to feel their softness, but they always purchased an unopened package.

"I make these sheets," the man whispered.

Irene's mouth just moved. She didn't know what to say.

"I'm the last person to see them before they leave the mill."

"Are you Inspector Number Five?" Irene blurted out.

The man lost some of his determined look. "I'm Number Seven. We work different shifts."

"Number Five inspected my sheets."

The man pulled harder at the skin under his chin.

"Do you know what Number Five looks like?"

"Different shift."

"Do you know his name?"

"Don't know him. Might even be a woman. Plenty of women work at the mill. All I know is that there is an Inspector Number Five. And I'm Number Seven. See my number gives you an idea about me. I mean, about my name. Go ahead, guess it."

"What? I couldn't. I...."

"It's Lucky. Number Seven. Seven days in a week. Lucky. Get it? Tells you something about me. The number five says nothing."

"But you said you wanted to be a truck driver," Irene said in defense of Number Five.

"Who's to say what's lucky." He scratched all of the fingers of his right hand down his chin to the base of his throat. "I just thought it would be nice to see where my work was going. You know, the way a truck driver takes his shipment to the end of the line." He looked at his hands. They became strangely silent and still.

Irene noticed that his hands were covered with liver spots. They reminded her of a pattern she had once seen on some bed linens.

"Never done this before. Just wanted to meet someone who uses my sheets. Just wanted to have someone in mind as I watch them passing by all day."

"I use them," Irene said softly.

Then again there was silence. The man stared at Irene a long time. He stared the way a hungry person might stare into an icebox empty of everything except an old head of iceberg lettuce.

He didn't rub his hands or pull at the skin under his chin.

The linens formed a colorful sea about them. Irene and the man waited in the silence like sleepers. Irene imagined she heard the sound of her heart in her ears the way her mother would describe it when her blood pressure was too high. Only to Irene, it was more like one long rumbling.

"Yes. That's it," he finally said as if whispering a toast. Then he stopped looking at her in the way a person might stop looking at something he wanted to remember. He stared back at the sheets. It was sort of a test. As if he wanted to remember her face without the help of sight.

The first thing Irene did after the man left was go to the towel wall. She started refolding the towels so that they fit perfectly in line. Nan came up beside her to help. Irene tried to tell Nan about the slip of paper she had found at home that read "Inspected by Number Five," and how the old man had been Inspector Number Seven. But Nan just stared at her and smiled the way she might smile in passing into one of the oval mirrors on the cosmetic counter downstairs.

"Those crazy folks will cut your brain into pieces," Nan said. "Probably just heard you say something about that silly Number Five business and it got his nut juices flowing. I heard on television that baked potatoes help absorb crazy juices."

Irene smiled and nodded in agreement. She wanted to tell Nan how fine linens washed over time become brighter and brighter more resembling light. But she felt uncomfortable as if someone had put a closed sign on the small door of their friendship.

Standing by her bed that night, Irene stared at the sheets. They seemed to almost glow with invitation. Somehow they had regained their dignity. Her hand gently brushed her hair. Her other hand placed the tiny strip of paper under her pillowcase like a child's tooth.

She climbed onto the bed and lay back on the sheets as if she were immersing herself in a bath filled by a stream of warm water. She pushed her hair back from her forehead. She heard the rumbling sound again. It was almost like water gurgling out of a bath and rushing in at the same time. And she knew that her linens were the soul of her home.

GULF

Martha lived alone in a trailer in Destin, Florida, on Highway 98. She was thirty-one. She would sit in the trailer watching wrestling matches on TV all night and work at the pier selling frozen shrimp for bait all day. Martha was afraid she would try to do her laundry at the post office or mail her letters to her father in the washing machine.

"People have a limited capacity for tragedy," Martha told Ceil, her neighbor. "Mine is limited like the number of shrimp you get on a seafood platter."

Ceil sat up in an E-Z Go golf cart in front of her trailer with the dignity of one of those ladies who sit up all night in airports waiting on mythical flights. The golf cart sat up on concrete blocks. "When you live alone you see little things add up in big damages."

"It's so silly," Martha continued. "I think how meaningless everything has become except for two or three things."

The pier was a distraction. For seventy-five cents a day, tourist daddies would leave their children to fish with Snoopy rods and reels, haul in croakers and bash their fishness and brains on the warm, dark planks until they returned from drinking draft beer to unhook them. Throughout the distance of the pier and the heat, Martha could hear it, the gurgled croaking of the fish and the bamm bamm bamm.

There was not much to do in Destin. People walked, fished and swam in the surf. Most people stayed for short periods of time. But there were the old women who seemed to have always been there. Martha watched them on the beach searching for sand dollars. They were happy women wearing large straw hats and the whitest clothes Martha had ever seen.

The old women made the largest sand dollars into clocks and painted the faces in bright acrylic flowers. The perfect, smaller ones they framed on red velvet above a card that told of the legend of the sand dollar.

On Martha's day off, she would follow them up the beach. She would imagine that the old women were giant sea birds picking the shoreline clean. They discarded the tiny, broken sand dollars. Sometimes Martha would pick up the rejected ones and carefully place them into the cups of her bikini top against her small breasts and let the salt water wash them out.

On Martha's birthday, she called her father. "I like to be alone at night and water my lawn," her father's voice said.

Martha turned on the TV. It was time for *The Andy Griffith Show.* Andy and Barney were looking through a box full of stuff from their old high school days. And Barney came up with a rock, and looked at it a long time in silence and said, "You know what this is?" And Andy said, "What?" "My dad's rock," Barney said. And they both looked at that dumb rock, and then Barney explained that his dad used to strike matches on it when he was a little boy, and he would watch him.

Martha asked Ceil about things.

"Discipline is what it takes," Ceil said. "I had a small insurance policy on my Horace when he totaled the Cadillac. I booked a tour of Europe, a series of teas and playgoing. I wasn't impressed. The passion plays were boring. All that stood out to me was Venice, Italy. The thing that excited me the most was something I found in the back of one of those world famous boutiques."

Ceil left her post in the golf cart, took Martha inside her trailer and handed her a small glass object. Inside, two green alligators were on a seesaw. There was a beach scene in the background with a sun Martha couldn't tell was rising or setting.

Ceil shook Martha's hand that held the paperweight so that a snowstorm began. White flakes fell slowly making the seesaw go up and down. *Florida* was inscribed on it. "At first I thought it was just a funny souvenir to find in a Venice gift shop. Then it struck me that it was some kind of a sign. When I returned, I sold my house and its memories and moved straight down the highway to Florida. Now I pass my time placing bets on which side of the seesaw will finish on top."

Ceil pointed to some shelves and Martha could see hundreds of neatly stacked glass paperweights. "That's what I mean by discipline," Ceil said.

Martha and Ceil walked to the beach. They stood in the sand with the water up to their necks, so that their bobbing heads looked like fishermen's floats.

"My father used to bring me to the beach and blow the ocarina until morning," Martha said.

"What's an ocarina?"

"It resembles something like a sweet potato." Martha pretended to hold one and mouthed three shrill toots. "My father and I'd talk between numbers. I remember walking with him and pointing out floating condoms. He'd say they were balloons from party boats. For a long time after that I imagined a fabulous Gulf of Mexico brimming over with ships decorated with crepe paper flags and balloons. I even asked my father if I could have my next birthday party on one of the boats."

"My father was just the opposite," Ceil said. "There was the time in New York at the Thanksgiving Day Parade. A 60-foot-long balloon moose passed over our heads, wagging in the breeze, lurching ever closer to the street. It took thirty people to handle it. They wore green ribbons that read, Inflation Team.

"The next morning, my father took me down to 36th and 7th to watch them take Bullwinkle apart. All the balloons I ever deflated had simply rocketed violently off, emitting sounds you wouldn't want to make in church, but the workmen slowly wound the ropes connecting the balloon down on sticks — an antler, a leg at a time. Bullwinkle slowly lost his moosey features."

Martha started playing one of those tunes that somehow sounds like it ought to be familiar yet isn't on her imaginary ocarina; Ceil cupped her hands and pretended to play an ocarina, too. Then they both just leaned back into the water, feeling like balloons whose mooring lines are being cast off one by one.

TV Guide

Ray took our TV.

He came home after work and caught me watching it alone. That was not the deal. I could watch it when he was with me. He thought I was obsessed. He thought the bald man on the TV-rental commercial was giving me special coded messages of love over the airwaves.

I woke up late the next morning. In place of the TV sat a large green bird in a cage. The thought of it terrified me. Ray knew what would bring me the most pain.

I paced the floor like a trapped animal, waiting for Ray to return home. I did not go near the birdcage. I expected some kind of explanation. There was none.

Ray ate his man-size, beefsteak TV dinner. His greasy lips did not speak a word.

That night I dreamed Ray and I were listening to one of those answer-man type radio programs and eating fried chicken. Ray thought I should listen more to the radio and less to TV. He tried to make a joke saying that it would make me less stationary. A woman caller was speaking on the radio. She said, "I only feel alive when I'm eating sunflower seeds in front of the pigeons at the park." There was static. The host of the radio show was explaining how you had to turn your radio off or at least down in volume before calling in your question. Ray was eating a chicken wing that didn't look very well-done. He gave out with a choking laugh. Then he fell facedown into the Barrel-O-Chicken and died right there. The next thing in the dream, I'm at the grocery store buying a cart-full of frozen chicken parts. I mean, I've got this passion for them.

I awoke to what sounded like Ray having an orgasm. It was not a loud thing, just a little sound like someone saying one of the vowels with the exception of Y. I felt around on top of me; he wasn't there. All was quiet, except for a peculiar scratching sound.

I descended the stairs. A light shone from the den. I knew I never left a light on. I peeked around the corner of the doorway in order to see something.

It was Ray. He was trying to teach the bird to talk. He had my copy of *The World's Best Loved Quotations*. Ray had given it to me to help me utilize my time better. He was reading through it to see which one the bird might like. "'Between grief and nothing I will take grief,'" he said softly to the bird. "That's Faulkner, a novelist." His fingers grazed the bars of the cage. I was pained to see how familiar they were.

The next morning Ray went to work without breakfast, without repeating his old joke about how Corn Chex was the national cereal of Czechoslovakia, and I just sat and listened to the water drip through the Mr. Coffee filter.

I decided to take the bird back to the pet shop where Ray had purchased it. I found the receipt in his sock drawer.

It was a small store called Fins, Furs, and Feathers. The cages were stuck among the rubber bones and doggie shampoos. A sign above the cages read, The Ideal Pet.

The saleswoman seemed too large for the store. She said she always loved birds. In her hand she held a napping bird. It looked dead.

As she returned the cage back among the others, she asked me if she looked eighty-seven years old. I said she didn't. It was the truth. She had these real good bones, the kind you know are hard just by looking at them.

"The secret to youth," she said, "is transcending the physical, ESP." She looked at the birdcages. All the birds seemed to come to life with song. It sounded like music you wanted to hear inside only and nowhere else.

I thought about how that kind of communication could change my life.

With the refund, I bought another TV. It wasn't near as nice as the original set. It had initials carved in the simulated wood frame. It didn't have remote control. But I didn't want to waste time shopping around.

Ray got home late that night.

I was in the kitchen making ham sandwiches. It's what I usually did whenever there was trouble. After wrapping all the sandwiches in plastic wrap, I put them in the freezer. Ray would have lunch made for weeks, I thought.

Ray entered the kitchen.

I was just sitting at the table, feeling for dead skin on my scalp, and waiting for the automatic dishwasher to shut off so I could check the stainless for spots.

"What would you have me do if you had your way?" he asked.

I said nothing. I stared at him with the silence of animals. I wanted to be restored by the silence, to restore Ray, to restore our home.

Ray put his hand on my knee. "We have to have a little realism around here," he said.

Something about that word realism smacked me like a board across the heart.

The hand stroking my knee seemed larger than I'd ever realized.

It was ten o'clock. It was time for the newscast. I opened us both a beer. On the TV something important was being said. I turned off the sound. Ray and I stretched out on the couch. For a moment, I thought about the things that might have spilled between the cushions over the years: pencils, coins, matches, combs.

Ray patted my hair. The couch was warm. The vinyl stuck to my skin. Ray's movements blurred in the grey light of the TV. His face became a cloudy image. I clung hard to him. I tried to kiss him.

"What's wrong?" he asked.

"I love you, too," I said.

ℱATHERS

At one time he worked in a small, sad barbershop all alone. It was not far from where my mother and I lived. When I needed a haircut, she would send me to him.

The only things personal about the shop were an old circus poster and his smell, which remained on his barber's smock after he was dead and made me cry as much as the knowledge that I would soon forget him.

My father would place his hands on both sides of my head as if he were making a tiny frame for my face. He wouldn't say anything. Barbering took him past speech. He would just look in the mirror at me. And I would look in the mirror at him, too. I would notice the way the mock crewneck collar of his smock made him look like a priest. He would run his fingers through my hair like a thick comb, still staring in the mirror at me, but he would never tell me what he saw.

There was nothing to do with me after the haircut, except to go over to the Kottage Restaurant for their vegetables. They were fresh, and you could get three with any dinner. My father said he brought my mother there once, but they gave her an eating utensil that wasn't too clean.

Amidst the sprinkles of sugar crystals on the tablecloth and the salt and pepper shakers that didn't match, my father would tell me his father's story. "My father," he would say, "was a great man. Short and bald, but still a champion gymnast. They would launch him out of the circus cannon with a puff of smoke 60 feet through the air, and always

73

he was caught safely. From the net he would leap to his feet to stand for the ovation of the crowd.

"How he did it not even I knew. Maybe it was a giant coiled spring and a huge firecracker? My mother wouldn't let him show me how. She wanted me to have a real career." My father stirred his coffee; the teaspoon sounded like a bell clapper. He smiled at his own foolishness.

"Once he let me climb atop his cannon," my father continued, gesturing with the pepper shaker. "But he never ever let me slip down the barrel."

Then we would walk to the cashier and wait for the waitress to come forward to tell the cashier what we had bought. The waitress wore a black shiny apron over a dingy white nylon dress. I wouldn't look at her, but I knew what she looked like anyway.

My father would say, "Better finish trimming your hair. Can't let you leave with your hair shaped like a Christmas tree." He would take me back and sit me in his chair. He would clip the ends of a few hairs with scissors, simply to keep me from leaving him. And I would look at the circus poster and think about his father, and how my father's story of his father was like having a familiar music box that didn't have to be opened for you to hear the music.

Finally, before I had to go, he would take a bottle of hard candy out of a half-empty drawer and offer me some. It was sad, the taste of the candy and the way the candy stuck together.

FOREIGN POSTCARD

Your postcard came today. I don't care to make a great nuisance over what is finished. It does not matter to me now. Once it did. I'll think about it very briefly then forget about it.

The postcard does not show clams waiting in a large bowl on a cutting table. If it did, I could imagine the clams softly opening and closing like the hundreds of secret things we should have revealed.

If that were the postcard, I could imagine you sent it to remind me to go shopping. "Don't forget to buy groceries," you'd say. "Don't forget to eat." But there are no clams giving up their grip on life in the postcard you sent.

What you sent me is a postcard of a train arriving or departing in Ecuador, an anachronism with highly polished Victorian brass, enormous amounts of escaping steam, and extravagantly costumed attendants. It is a first class view with all those cute and lovable ponchoed Indians attractively displayed in the brown landscape. It is a lazy and bastard card that will never increase your wisdom or mine. The inscription reads, "It's a beginning."

It is not the real departure or arrival. The one where hundreds of passengers bleed into the cars, tearing hair, not fitting, and hundreds of others try to get out of the cars, smashing themselves with huge baskets, jabbing steel umbrellas into dandruffed shoulders, and sliding into tunnels of rain-beaded orphans, Indian farmers, and clowns in half make-up.

The postcard doesn't show the train stops where young prostitutes club guinea pigs to death with broom handles, or a kid in a blue hat pushing an empty wheelbarrow over stone pavement dotted with manure, stops to look at you, then into the sun before falling down in a spasm, curled in a slapping, vomiting ball.

The postcard doesn't show what I would do if I were with you. I would take you to a restaurant where all over the tables lie jigsaws of dried food particles spilt from countless servings before. As if reading an ancient tablet, I would show you the messages of what was eaten in the place during the wet or dry years. It would be a history of good and bad harvests. We would inspect microcosms of rice, beans, cheese, and wine. And I would wonder why you bothered to ask the waiter for a menu.

We would hear the whistle blow. You would board the train. The train would jerk into motion, and a moment later your waving figure would abruptly be yanked around a curve and into the past, leaving me to wonder if you can even get clams in Ecuador.

THE APPLIANCES OF LOSS

Dan sat in the living room, watching the late show on TV. He stretched his legs, adjusted the waistband of his Sears boxer shorts, and leaned back in his well-worn La-Z-Boy recliner. He thought about how for some reason you could hardly ever get anything worth watching anymore, even on Saturday night, even on cable. That thought made him not worry so much about not having a color set.

The black and white TV had been a gift from Dan's mother. She had been complaining for years about how the kids should come back home and clean out all of the Chubby Checker limbo albums and the Mr. Potato Head sets of their youth. But when Dan loaded up the old TV into the station wagon, his Mom changed her mind. As Dan's automobile left the driveway, his mom hung hard to the front of the hood, like a hunter's trophy.

Dan could not see driving the six hours from Tallahassee to Atlanta staring at his mother's face, haloed by the sun, through his windshield. He stopped the car a block from her house. He asked her what was wrong. It was then that she told Dan how the television set had killed his father.

"We had just looked in the *TV Guide,*" Dan's mother had said. "We had agreed to watch the Bob Hope special. There would be no argument. Your father stood up and pushed back his TV tray. I remember he was eating fried chicken. Your father had chosen to buy the chicken at Kentucky Fried. It was Regular Recipe style. They hadn't invented Extra Crispy yet. He walked up to the TV and turned it on. No picture, just a funny little light in the middle of the screen."

Dan pulled the back door of the station wagon down so his mother could have a place to sit.

"Your father knew it was the tube. He rushed out to the store," Dan's mother continued. "He bought a new Motorola. The man in the store took your father's check. He helped your father load the TV onto the front seat. But as your father started to shift the car into drive, he had a heart attack. The man at the appliance store called to tell me about it. I came down to pick up the car. The new TV set was still sitting on the front seat. The man in the store said no refunds."

Dan looked at the TV sitting up in the back of the station wagon. Dan's mother pointed at the set and said, "That's the very TV that killed him."

Dan felt miserable, but he needed a TV. He wished his father had gone out to buy a toaster that day. Dan already had a good toaster.

The movie showing on the late show was about a hatchet murderer. The police had caught him after he had hacked the legs off dancers at a roller-disco party. He was still circling the rink in a pair of those skates with the nice pom-poms when the police broke in and shot him in the head.

The police took him to the morgue, thinking he was dead. But as the attendant was putting him in the cooler, the hatchet murderer's hand started swaying as if the hatchet were still in it.

"Honey," Sue, Dan's wife, said, interrupting the movie, "you want something to eat before I cut the kitchen light off?"

"Nothing, dear," Dan answered.

"I can scramble up some eggs. I can use that Pam cooking spray. It doesn't have the calories or fat of butter." Dan's wife had been seriously considering her diet.

"No food," Dan said. "Come on and watch this movie with me."

"You won't catch me dead watching that kind of movie. I'm just going to sit in the tub awhile."

Sue leaned over and kissed him on his bald spot. "You want any tonight," she said, "you better come to bed soon."

"Sure, babe," Dan said, his eyes still fixed on the TV set.

After the movie was over, Dan decided that he would get a snack from the kitchen.

Dan smiled at the new magnets that his wife had put on the refrigerator door. One read, "Put the blitz on fat." Another read, "Be a member of the Why Not Be Thin Club." Sue had gotten the magnets in her Quickly Slim Diet Powder box. The powder was supposed to turn on her body's natural fat burners as easy as turning on the oven. The box promised an all-out war against stubborn bulges, and it promised to actually shrink fat cells. Photos on the box showed the before and after appearance of a Staten Island woman who had lost an amazing ninety-five pounds. The copy under the photos also said that the weight loss had helped her catch a new husband. Dan wondered if that meant she had gotten rid of her old husband.

Dan opened the refrigerator door. He noticed something different pushed behind the Tupperware bowls of leftovers. It was not the usual turkey or ham loaf. On the back of the top shelf, illuminated by the tiny refrigerator light, was the body of a small animal. Half of the animal had no fur on it, so that the pink muscles of the thighs, the hindquarters, and the belly were visible along with the bluish membrane attaching the skin to the flesh.

Dan decided against the snack. He closed the door. He turned the kitchen lights off. He walked into the bedroom. He got under the covers and fluffed up his favorite pillow, the one that had somehow been pressed thinner than the rest of the pillows over the years.

Dan put his hands behind his head and leaned back. He stared at the tiny cracks in the plaster. He could still hear the water splashing about Sue in the tub as she turned the pages of a magazine. He looked towards the bathroom and saw Sue getting out of the water, pulling the plug from the drain. She noticed him and began posing with a towel. Then she looked in the full-length mirror. She lifted one of her buttocks with her hand and let it drop. "I could really stand to shed some more pounds," she said.

"You're special already," Dan said.

"It's not easy losing weight. I don't like eating vegetables."

"What about a nice salad for lunch?" Dan tried to be encouraging.

"Dan, you know what lettuce tastes like to me."

"Dirt?"

"Dirt."

"What about some exercise?" Dan asked, and pointed to the bed.

"I think I get more than enough of that kind of exercise," she said.

Later that night, Dan had a dream. He saw Sue cutting the skin off of a large animal with a long knife. The knife reminded Dan of the one that the local butcher used. This made Dan feel uneasy. Anything associated with the local butcher made Dan feel uneasy. Once the butcher had shaken Dan's hand and the butcher's hand had been freezing cold. The butcher had previously been shaping some ground pork patties to look like little pigs. He used raisins to make tiny pig faces on the lumps of ground meat. Dan did not know of these activities. He just thought how oddly cold the butcher's hands were, and somehow the thought of it made Dan stop going to the butcher's shop.

In the dream, Sue slit the flesh of the animal along each thigh, and she removed the skin in a rolling manner similar to the way one takes off a sock. She then detached the delicate bluish membrane attaching the skin of the animal to its flesh, so that just the bare pink muscle showed. Then, Sue started laughing and covering her nude body with blood from a white bowl that lay at her feet. Finally the face of the animal became visible. It was his own.

Dan sat up in bed as if a Big Ben alarm clock had gone off inside him. He shook Sue's shoulder. "Dear," he said. He shook her again. Her eyes opened. "I was wondering," he said. "What's that animal body doing in our refrigerator?"

Sue moved closer to him. She placed his hand on her breast. "I ran over Emily's cat in the car yesterday. I was late for my reducers' club meeting. I didn't know what to do. I put the body in the refrigerator until I could think of how to tell her. I'll take care of it tomorrow."

Dan felt bad for having made Sue explain things. He let her go back to sleep. He thought about buying her one of those digital bathroom scales that kept a record of how much you had weighed the last time you stepped on it. He wondered if he could purchase one with some trading stamps they had been saving from the gas station. He wondered if he would miss the wheel on the old scale in the bathroom and the way its numbers flashed back and forth until it stopped on the proper weight.

The next morning at breakfast, Dan said that he would go by and explain about the cat to Emily, but Sue said that she would take care of it after work. Dan finished his Nutri-Grain cereal. He did not think about the cat again until later that evening.

As Dan was driving home, a block from his house, he saw Emily, his neighbor, tacking up lost cat signs on the telephone poles. Dan waved to her. He thought about pulling over and telling Emily about the accident, but he felt he should let Sue tell her in her own way.

Sue was sitting in the kitchen when Dan came through the door. Sue was smiling and wearing her favorite red dress. Dan liked to call it The Perfect Dress. He liked the way it was cut so that it showed off Sue's shoulder bones. They both agreed that her best feature was her flawless, smooth shoulders. Dan wondered why he hadn't seen Sue in her favorite dress in so long a time.

Sue grabbed Dan by the hand and led him to the bathroom. She stood on the old scales and pointed to the dial where the numbers were spinning. The numbers stopped at 126.

Dan could feel that number carried a great deal of weight with Sue. "I've lost five pounds," Sue said with the kind of enthusiasm one would normally expect to hear only from cured lepers.

"What?" Dan said.

"Five pounds. It was that cat. I've hardly touched any food in the refrigerator since I put the cat in there."

"Yes," Dan said, "that cat. You've got to tell Emily. She's outside putting up lost cat posters. She's probably worrying herself sick."

"Five pounds," Sue said with the increased confidence that sudden weight loss brings.

Dan felt guilty as they drove past Emily on their way to Momma and Poppa's. Sue wanted Italian food and dancing, maybe a glass of wine. Emily was still putting up posters. And that night, back at home, Sue decided she wanted to be on top for a change. She no longer felt she had to lie flat on her back to make her stomach seem smooth.

The next morning, Dan demanded that Sue tell Emily about her cat while he was at work or else he would tell her when he came home. But when Dan came home all he found was a note from Sue that read,

"Lost five more. My life has to change. I've come to realize that there isn't room enough in my world to keep everything."

He looked around the house. The charge cards that were usually in his top drawer were gone. The old weight scale in the bathroom was gone. The Perfect Dress was gone. There were travel magazines beside the phone with their pages dog-eared down on photos of exotic beach resorts.

Dan went to the refrigerator. The magnets were gone. He opened the door. The cat body was no longer there. Dan looked at the empty box of Quickly Slim Diet Powder. He thought again about how that Staten Island woman had caught a new husband.

Dan walked next door to Emily's house. He thought at least Sue would have told her something when she returned the cat. He rang the bell.

Emily invited him in. He asked if she had seen Sue. Emily told Dan that she hadn't seen Sue for days. Dan noticed the copies of *Cat Fancy* magazine scattered across the living room. Emily divined what he was looking at.

Emily explained to Dan about her missing cat. Dan said nothing. Emily said that she was looking for a picture of a cat that looked like her little Skippy. She wanted to have something to take with her around the neighborhood and show door-to-door. The idea of taking a picture of a cat that resembled the lost cat door-to-door somehow reminded Dan of the reruns of *Cannon*, a portly detective who liked to drive around Los Angeles in a shiny Continental searching for fine cuisine. Dan looked across the room. He noticed that Emily had a large screen, color TV with remote control. Dan promised Emily that he would be happy to help her look for her lost Skippy.

Later that evening, as Dan and Emily were sharing popcorn and watching an old episode of *Hawaii Five-O,* Dan told Emily about how Sue had lost weight and left him for a more dramatic social life. Dan did not mention the cat. For all he knew his wife had that cat crammed in some styrofoam cooler down in Florida. Dan and Emily wept together over their losses.

After a few Caribbean postcards from Sue, Dan moved in with Emily. Even though he was good about doing the largest or the smallest tasks about the house, Emily could never figure out why Dan would never open her refrigerator door. But Dan knew, and he wasn't taking any chances.

Several months later, Dan sold his own house, and, even though he had no complaints about its unrelenting operation, he sold the black and white television set that had killed his father. He only watched color now. There was nothing else he could do.

ALICE STORIES

THE SHOEBOX OF DESIRE

Alice and I ate dinner in her kitchen. After coffee, she pulled out her shoebox of real life stories of fertility and desire. She cut them out of newspapers and magazines. She saved them until someone visited, then she read them aloud.

Alice scratched the polish off her nails while she spoke.

The first clipping was about a woman who had crabs, but didn't know. She thought she had caught fleas from her cat. She tried dusting herself with flea powder. Then an article appeared in a leading woman's magazine that explained about the crabs epidemic.

The woman was dating a married man. She hoped to give them to him, to give to his wife. She hoped this would make the wife leave him. She wanted to marry the man. It never happened.

Another story was about a phobia in China called *shook-yong*. A man believed that his penis would disappear into his abdomen and that he would die. To prevent this, he gripped his penis firmly. When he grew tired, his wife, friends, and relatives lent a hand. A specialist constructed a wooden clasp and recommended his wife apply fellatio immediately. The victim's spirits were lifted.

Many other young men have since been accused of feigning *shook-yong*.

The final story was about a man who won a free dinner for two. He won it on a flight from Atlanta for having the oldest penny on the plane. He didn't think he had a chance to win. The penny was dated 1964.

The man did not know anyone in San Francisco to eat with.

On the way to his motel the man thought he saw some cobalt blue Depression-era glass at a yard sale. He got out of his rental car and examined things. He lit a cigarette. He picked up a pigeon-blood vase.

The house looked empty.

A woman came down the sidewalk carrying a grocery bag. She had tremendous thighs.

"Hello," she said to the man.

"I thought no one was here," he said.

"It's a pretty good vase," she said and put down the bag.

"How much?"

"Make me an offer," she said and pulled out two cans of beer. She gave the man one.

"Is it a copy?" he asked.

"A copy?" She laughed. "Two things I grabbed when my dad threw me out and chased me down the street, that vase and a big box of Kotex."

"He threw you out?"

"I drank a little wine. Kept it in that vase. Nothing wrong in that, but I was scared of my dad. I feared him. He seldom put his hand on me, but his look, just his look, was enough to tell me I had better keep quiet and take what was coming to me. A lot of times I'd just as soon he slapped me in the face than look at me that way."

The woman also told the man that as a child she had been so beautiful that she had once been mistaken for a princess. She said that she had been such a young bride that she played with dolls. And she told once again how her dad had chased her down the street with her carrying the vase and the sanitary napkins, only this time she mentioned another man and a shotgun.

88

The man told the woman about the free dinner tickets. He asked if she would like him to pick her up later in the rented car.

I thanked Alice for the food and stories. She asked me what I thought they all meant. I said that maybe desire isn't conditional. She agreed, but I'm not sure she understood. I'm not sure I understood.

We decided to have more coffee.

ℒ𝔦fe Story

Alice was trying to tell her life story at the same pace at which a dying man's life is said to pass in review before his eyes.

"My father," she said, "caught a mouse one day, tied a little string around his neck, and I walked it up and down the street.

"I took it by my grandmother's. She lived in a red-brick house. It had tall chimneys and a garden of blood-colored roses. I don't remember much about her except her size. I liked to watch and see if she'd be able to rise from her chair.

"In my grandmother's dining room there was a glass-fronted cabinet and in the cabinet a few black feathers and the skeleton of a bird.

"I asked my grandmother about it. She told me how the blackbird had flown through my grandfather's office window, busting the glass and killing itself. The blackbird's fatal flight plan cut off the top of its skull. It flopped in shards of glass on his desk, frantically beating broken wings. It trembled and died.

"Grandfather took sick at once. A janitor was called to sweep up the debris. Grandfather went home.

"Grandfather's voice grew faint as a soft wind. In his mind the bird's death was a curse. He put the blame on a woman who wanted to get on a bus he once drove for a previous job.

"The woman tried to take a chicken and a goat on the bus with her. 'Sorry, no goats,' my grandfather told her. 'Since when no goats?' she asked. 'I never let goats ride,' he said. 'What about the chicken?' 'Chickens are O.K.'

"The woman handed the goat's lead rope to a waiting child. The chicken flew from the woman's arm into the bus, defecating all the way to the back. 'One more question,' the woman began, but before she could gather her breath to utter it, Grandfather said the answer to all questions that shouldn't be asked, 'To get to the other side.'

"There was sharp silence for a moment, then a ripple of delayed laughter struck the passengers on the bus. The woman did not laugh with them, but let out a short scream like that of squeaky-bed wheels being moved or someone weeping and dying. Then she ran away in the direction the child had taken the goat.

"After that Grandfather acted strange. He would no longer drive the bus. He thought the thorns on the roses looked like bird beaks. He took a desk job in a tall office building.

"I liked to stick what was left of the feathers into the skeleton to try and make the bird look real. I always pestered Grandmother for them. I never wanted anything as much as I wanted those feathers and bones.

"When Grandmother died, I thought, 'Now I can have the black-bird.' But my father said, 'Oh, those old feathers and bones. I'm afraid I threw them away.'

"I left school after the eighth grade. I worked for a while in a hospital. I emptied the patients' purses and took their urine samples to the lab.

"There was one woman's urine that looked thick as pudding. You could have cut it with a knife.

"This was the funniest part of my life. The place was a snake pit. They had one room for women. It was a big circle of beds.

"There was one woman there who said they locked her up because she couldn't find her mouth to eat with. She threw the food on her chest. But every day she'd still manage to put a little plate on the floor for her dog. When no one was looking, I'd pick the plate up and put it back on the table because I didn't want the doctors to know she was feeding a dog who wasn't there. The dog's name was Sue Sue.

"They brought another woman in. Someone had tried to cut her head off. She was slit from ear to ear. They locked her up in a special room. You could hear her banging her head off all night.

"What else can I tell you? I wanted to be married. I lived in an apartment with roaches everywhere. I kept a hammer in one hand. I bought fancy underwear. I was a virgin until my first wedding night although I allowed an orderly at the hospital once to put his hand under my whites.

"I thought I was pregnant once. The doctor said, 'Four months.' I told him I still had my period."

"I remember seeing two legs going up. I didn't know they were mine. I felt something scraping me. The doctor said, 'It isn't a pregnancy.'

"They held this thing in front of me on forceps. The doctor said it was my twin. It had gotten inside of me in my mother's womb. I wondered whether it would have been my brother or sister.

"Were it not ongoing, that might be a scene to remember. The one that offered the least satisfaction." Alice clicked her tongue, and then lit a cigarette.

I wondered about the point of Alice's story. I reminded myself that she had had two coronaries and three marriages. I guessed that some life stories don't have a point. The most beautiful ones are irrational gifts. And maybe a friend should know less about a friend after hearing her life story, not more.

STILL POINTS

Alice leaned in close and whispered, "You are not astonished enough by your own life." She was grinning. Her face was like a child's equation written on a blackboard.

Her nurse came in and gave her injections. While the nurse was away, Alice made friendly indecent proposals.

I thought about that Mexican girl who had hundreds of needles inside her. The newspaper said she didn't feel any pain until they emerged through the skin. A priest counted two-hundred and thirteen needles coming out of her buttocks, breasts, and insides of her thighs.

"I've decided to make a list of things that astonish me about my life," I said to Alice. The first thing I wrote down was that I watered plants long after they were dead.

Alice asked me to make sure her house shoes were placed in the right direction by her bed so she could step right into them.

"You know Jung's theory of synchronicity?" Alice asked. "That some things are both familiar and surprising?"

"Like the first time we had sex," Alice said.

"You notice one thing, today, like a lot of three-legged dogs, and you notice the same thing tomorrow." I wondered when the nurse would interrupt us again.

"After you die you probably realize you knew what it was going to be like all along." Alice put part of the chain from her St. Jude medal in her mouth.

I thought about my list again. I tried to note down something about my childhood, but I was not a success as a child.

My art teacher wanted me to draw realistic trees. She told me my green balls with little brown bases didn't look like any trees she'd ever seen. "But I've climbed them, hugged them, and fallen out of them," I said. Still, she gave me a sour look and a note to carry home to my parents.

After that incident I only drew realistic pictures of the sinking of the Titanic. Then the teacher left me alone. The little bow of the ship going down. The darkness. A couple of white lumps on top of the water for the iceberg because ninety-five percent of the iceberg was underwater. And little arms reaching up out of the water.

Alice put her hand on mine. I felt how soft and warm it was, and at the same time I felt the bones under her skin. I thought about how funny it was that we all had the same skeletal scaffolding and yet how different we looked on our fleshy surfaces.

Alice looked tired. She talked about the death of her children. She worried me, but it was on her mind. She told me of an abortion she had in Atlanta and the Greyhound bus ride home. She described the bus ride in detail, but not the abortion.

The wallpaper in the hospice room was pink. The floor lamp had a great dark pink shade. Old people, men and women, sat on a red sofa in the hall, their canes beside them, or between their legs. They did not talk. They seemed asleep.

Alice handed me a small black and white photograph. The picture was not of a person. It was of a small house. A little square of lawn. A driveway. Bricks and windows. "It's the house I was born in," Alice said. "There used to be a porch out back. My mother and I would sit on it and drink tea and imagine we were at a tea party given by the Mad Hatter in *Alice in Wonderland*. We would ask each other foolish

94

riddles that had no answers and sometimes we would engage in a Lobster Quadrille."

I looked at the photograph again. I longed to see the porch behind the house, but it was just a picture of the front.

"That house is gone now," Alice said. "In fact, all of the houses I've ever lived in are gone."

I understood the worn out feeling that comes with having outlived all of the important structures that framed your life.

Alice asked me how my list was coming. I read her my final entry. It was Eliot, "at the still point of the moving world." I told her how I tended to move towards still points.

"No," she said. "You can't end it that way. That would be a terrible ending."

I blinked to rid my eyes of tears and promised the way a politician does that I would find another ending.

TALES OF RUCAR

The Bear Tamers

It was enough that his father taught dancing bears to massage the muscles of poor people weary from working all day in the fields of Rucar. The elder of the tribe rubbed a pinch of salt on a small loaf of bread and tore it into two pieces. The bear tamer's son and I exchanged portions before eating them. We were married.

Our wedding night was enlivened by Bruin, his father's favorite. First my new husband bathed me in milk. Then I lay down on the floor to enjoy the bear's somewhat heavy-footed treatment. My husband beat time with his handmade drum. I intoned the prayer for starting a journey. My muscles tensed. They let go. Then I don't know what I did. But since then I have never been on particularly good terms with my orgasms.

When I was again among the living, my new husband smiled at me. A cigarette hung from his lips like a wolf's fang. The smoke was like the shadow of a pale angel.

About the subject of love, my grandmother said, "A man has a mouse in his trousers."

About the subject of bears, my grandmother said nothing.

I had lived with her in a place called The Street of Spoons. It was called The Street of Spoons because of the principal profession of the community. The people would collect wood in the forest and carve beautiful spoons out of it. Occasionally an eccentric would move into the area and make wooden combs.

In the autumn many of the women would work as farm laborers. The men preferred to stay closer to home. It was while returning from working on the land that I met the bear tamer and his son.

They were toiling along the road, dressed in leather coats studded with brass ornaments, dragging after them a big black bear. The men's tawny skin and faces were framed in locks of hair that fell like bluish-black snakes upon their necks.

It pleased the men to show off their bear to us. They put on heavenly smiles, disclosing their white teeth.

The older man started imitating castanets by cracking the joints of his fingers. He motioned for the younger to begin banging a drum. Then the older man threw his cap in the air and started strutting about like a peacock.

The bear did not pay much attention to the men beyond giving a low grunt.

The older man began to shout excitedly at it. He kicked its legs apart.

The bear rose up on its hind legs. It danced heavily. It was the sad dance of a tired bear on a hot, dusty road. But we applauded.

The men followed us back to The Street of Spoons to camp for the night.

The houses on The Street of Spoons were made of tree trunks joined by pieces of packing cases. They were only used in the wintertime or when there was rain. Most of the time we slept outdoors on skins.

That night my grandmother served the men Tuica with manaliga. The prune liqueur added a festive touch to the dry maize porridge. With a string, Grandmother cut the bear a large slice and even added some stewed fruit.

After our meal, my husband-to-be told me how they trained the bears. "We heat an iron tray," he said. "And when it is very hot, we set the bear upon it. We play music and beat a drum. The bear feels the heat and begins to hop. After a while, the bear learns to hop just to the rhythms of the drum."

Then he told me how they caught the bears in the mountains.

There were three things I had to do after my new husband and I lay down on the floor together.

One was to carry a lump of sugar under my armpit to ensure the sweetness of my wedding.

Second was to save the pieces of a plate that my husband broke behind me.

And the third, the most important thing of all, consecrated our carnal union.

My grandmother appeared at the door with a chicken in a sack. I thanked her and told her it would not be needed.

I danced on a table wearing a bloodstained garment. It was the proof my husband's family needed. It was a slow dance. I was tired and sore. All roared with laughter. The wine had gone to their heads.

I climbed down from the table and sat in one of the chairs that surrounded the revelers. The chair legs sank down into the ground. My new husband was drinking with the men and dancing as though possessed. It was like death.

Later someone suggested that the party move on to another house. Three fiddlers led the procession. Some of them carried torches.

I stayed behind with a man and a woman who were quarreling. He told her how he had cut his first wife's nose off for committing adultery. She said that that had seemed fair, but having her banished from the community seemed too harsh.

I heard the bears in the dark scratching paws and legs in an attempt to break their leashes. Or maybe, I thought, they were just practicing their daily leapings and slidings that took them nowhere.

I decided to make the bears more manaliga and stewed fruit, to learn all of their secret names.

About the subject of love, my grandmother said, "A woman marries her lips together."

The Church Of Summer Sausage

The man with big hands, the man whose fingers traced every precious inch of the textured sausages, knew that there were no sausages lovelier or more delicate in form than Anna's.

The man was barely breathing. On St. Ramfir's Day, the choice of sausage carried weight. It was the memory of last year's sausage, the peasants said, that helped put that old foot in front of that other old foot until the holy day arrived again.

Anna was haggling over the price of a chicken with an old woman who sold golden-brown rolls at the next booth. The rolls were sprinkled with honey and walnut. The old woman's breath smelled of breakfast toast.

Anna had brought a half dozen hens to market bound round her neck on a chain. When a bird was purchased, it was torn off the chain and given to the buyer. The remaining chicken heads formed a perfect inventory.

The chickens were only a sideline today. Normally, the market was filled with vegetables and fruit, which became less and less appetizing under the humid heat. What began in the luxuriance of red paprika and the masses of tomatoes piled in heaps beside the cartloads of watermelons ended in the somber stench of decay.

Anna turned to the man in front of her booth. She had sausages to sell before the procession of St. Ramfir's jawbone. "Something?" Anna asked.

"Who can bear these beautiful forms?" the man said. He exposed a set of teeth that could have invented love.

"Beauty looks for its own match," Anna said, admiring the splendidly embroidered cloak of the large man. He was a csikos, a guardian of the horses for a wealthy family.

Anna felt an insect pricking her, and would have lifted up her red muslin skirt to scratch her groin, but she wanted to keep the illusion of a mystery that didn't exist.

Anna's family numbered eight, and all slept on skins and straw on the ground in the same one-room hovel. Anna had her own corner and near her slept her sister and her brother-in-law. The ground was hard and the skins smelled. The insects in the skins would wait until the silent watches of the night, until all lay motionless. Then they would inflict their bites.

After Anna scratched fiercely, they would lead her to believe that she had destroyed them. For a moment she would feel free and her body would tingle gratefully. But then the stinging would begin again on her breasts or some different part of her body. Other times the irritation would take the form of a hand moving over her body. It was no sluggish hand, for it traveled straight towards her ragged undergarments. These beasts briefly succumbed to the scratches of her nails, too.

Anna thought about the wishbones in all the hens about her neck. She desired the skill to crack them in the right way. "Bacon makes bold," she said to the man as he selected a sausage.

He stared at her face and noticed how her thick eyebrows seemed to form an uninterrupted straight line. It was the only distinct feature above her slender upper torso. Then his gaze came to rest upon her rather full hips.

104

Anna seemed to divine his thoughts.

They were interrupted by the sound of the church bells that marked the beginning of the procession. A flight of doves was loosed. A band played. And a long line of priests and monks marched through the center of the market followed by the nuns veiled in black. Then a woman passed alone in front of the band, walking slowly and proudly. Her black dress was ornamented in gold lace. In her hands she carried the sculpted gold monstrance that contained the jawbone of St. Ramfir.

As the jawbone passed, the men and the women in the crowd took bites of sausage and handed pieces of sausages to their children. It was a gesture in honor of the man who gave them their church.

Anna loved to hear her father tell the story of how once in Rucar there lived a rich man who built a beautiful church of stone. The church was his pride, and neither the peasants of the village nor his wife was allowed to enter it. This made everyone angry and his wife stopped cooking for him.

The spiritual head of the village then was an old man named Ramfir who worked in the fields every day beside the other peasants. His heart was heavy with the thought that the people could not worship in the church. So, he talked the peasants into building their own church out of summer sausage right next to the church of stone.

At first the rich man would strut in front of the church of summer sausage. He would ask the peasants if they had ever seen a real church. But then a breeze would blow and bring to the rich man's nose the delicious scent of sausage, even more delicious since his wife had stopped preparing his meals.

At last the day came when the rich man had not enough strength to resist the temptation. He agreed to exchange with the peasants. As soon as he took possession of the appetizing church, he started straight away to nibble. The first week he ate the door. The second week he could not resist eating the pulpit. And in short time there was nothing left.

Because of St. Ramfir, the poor villagers who could hardly call their souls their own in those days were able to get a fine stone church to pray in.

As the jawbone of St. Ramfir passed Anna's booth, she held a tiny sausage tight and bit into it, tasting the organs together: the liver, the kidneys, and the red slippery heart.

The man waved the remains of his broken sausage. They were both silent. It was the silence that grew out of exact revelations. "Sweet as the showers of summer," he finally said.

Anna slipped her fingers around the chain that encircled her neck. She pulled the ring of hens over her head, but her straight black hair knotted in one link.

His large hands untangled the fine strands, then touched her lips.

The prickly movement under her skin was not like that caused by the insects.

His mustache stole, hair by hair, into her sight.

She was now all the texture that she wore. And he was the one she had anticipated. Beauty looked for its own match.

And suddenly the delicious scent of the summer sausage blurred her breath.

THE PLEASURE GARDEN
OF THE ROOT VEGETABLES

Vula's body no longer resembled the back of a breakfast chair.

Vula's father was glad. He twirled the silver ring on his little finger the way the strangers at the horse fair had twirled their huge mustachios.

Vula's mother brushed Vula's hair. Her hair was flying like a black waterfall.

At the fair, Vula's father had taken her to see the sword swallower. The thick sword slid down the old man's throat. It reminded Vula of the method tiny boys had for swallowing green lizards. The sword disappeared silently. It was the silence Vula's mother had warned her against.

The strange men at the fair had held Vula like a handsome piece of furniture. Her tears formed a curtain of beads over the door they had opened.

Vula's mother had stopped brushing Vula's hair.

Vula's father piled the silver coins on the table in front of her mother. The clinking sound was their only dialogue.

Vula's mother was a large woman. Her body had been toughened by having worked for years in the fields of root vegetables. Today, Vula's mother felt like a sad plant: no leaves, no vine, no flowers. A plant whose one fruit had become too hard to eat.

Vula's mother looked at her small husband. The men of Rucar did not need large frames for the work they did. Her eyes stared at him like the empty shells of mollusks found in upturned soil.

Vula's father understood the look her mother gave him. It was time to go to the Pleasure Garden of the Root Vegetables.

In Rucar, one thing is never done. No Rucarian will strike or injure a man below the waist. The seed of man is considered too precious to risk.

As St. Ramfir wrote in *The Book of Feathers*, "A man's spear of destiny glows like the sacramental chalice and a woman's breasts are scripture." St. Ramfir had worked many years beside the peasants in the fields of Rucar and understood the desire that jangled softly in front of their bellies.

The Book of Feathers is a small book. Church history has it that St. Ramfir was walking in a field of potatoes when above him he saw a white crow. The white crow was soon attacked by a flock of ordinary crows. It fell at St. Ramfir's feet. With the bones and feathers of this crow, St. Ramfir covered what was later to be called *The Book of Feathers*. It is the book that contains all of the Rucarian rules for spiritual fighting.

St. Ramfir's vision in the field was of the Pleasure Garden of the Root Vegetables. It would be the only place in Rucar where violence would be acceptable. The Pleasure Garden would be an open field surrounded by 27 tables, each of which would be covered with food and drink. And, in the very center of the field, there would be one table covered only with root vegetables and the bones of crows and other birds.

Early church history held that the table in the center of the Pleasure Garden represented the white crow and that the 27 tables surrounding the field stood for the number of ordinary crows in the attacking flock. Other people thought that 27 was just a number St. Ramfir enjoyed counting up to.

Vula and her family entered the Pleasure Garden of the Root Vegetables. The rest of the tribe had followed them to the field. The followers busied themselves by filling up the 27 tables with black bread, ham, cutlets, peppers, gherkins, and bottles of Tuica.

Vula's father and mother moved to the center table. Each stood on separate sides of the pile of bones and vegetables. Vula stood by her mother.

The tribe lit the 27 lamps surrounding the Pleasure Garden. The hiss of the blue flames cursed the darkening sky.

Vula's mother clenched a potato so tightly in her fist that when she released it from her grip it was crushed into a mash. She worked herself into a naked passion and then suddenly fired a potato at her husband's minuscule form.

In moments of trial like this it was proper for the rest of the tribe to maintain a fierce and dogged silence. But many of the women in the tribe could feel a secret, silent language scratching in their throats.

Vula's father picked up the bones of a small bird and hurled them back towards Vula's mother. It was a desperate sight to see the mere skeletons of birds flying through the air without the aid of wing or feather.

Bones and vegetables, illuminated by the blue flames, flashed across the table like the ghostly shadows of past meals.

Their throws began to take on fancier flourishes and more structural accuracy; it was as if the very food itself was taking out its own revenge for being pulled from the earth or plucked from the sky.

Finally, Vula took up a firm potato in the palm of her hand. She launched it straight into her father's eye. He crumpled to the ground. Things came to a halt.

Vula and her mother lifted him back onto his feet. The potato had been a small, innocent thing that had reminded Vula's father of the pain that comes to everyone in different forms. The pain in his eye moved him past speech.

He embraced his daughter and wife. He led them to one of the 27 tables and served them generous portions of meat, and poured their drink, and buttered their bread on both sides, and, in this way, asked their forgiveness.

Then the tribe became ferocious over the unexpected beauty found in the way Vula and her mother chewed the food served to them. And they all came before the substantial tables. And they all drank and ate so well that in the morning only the gleaming bones of birds and a few potatoes were left to replenish the table at the center of the Pleasure Garden of the Root Vegetables.

$\mathcal{O}$HE $\mathcal{L}$AMPSHADE $\mathcal{V}$ENDOR

It was typical. The door was open. It was summer. The TV was on.

A white-haired man dressed in a black and frayed tuxedo came to the door selling lampshades. He was a dignified man transformed by the loss of his hands. He picked up a shade with one of his metal claws. "Sell you a new lampshade?"

I didn't like the shade. I had never even given much thought to the lampshades I already had. I wondered how he lost his hands. I tried to make conversation. "A man knocked on the door yesterday selling mops and brooms. Do you know him?"

He put the lampshade back on his cart. "No relation. I sell shades. You want one?"

I've always loved human activities that are on the way out. I asked him how long he had sold lampshades.

"Fifteen years ago, I had a sideshow at all the big fairs, a flea circus. But I was hit hard by hygiene and taste."

"I saw a flea circus once, but no one believes me," I said. "I keep it to myself. But I'd swear I remember a tiny flea wedding and a flea riding on a bicycle."

"I had a little table for the stage, and I would only allow a few chairs for the audience," the man continued. "I had a ballet sequence, a tightrope walk, and a wagon train race. The secret was all in the human flea. They are the only ones with the necessary power to tug and push with their back legs. My fleas were incredible. What stamina. They could perform hundreds of shows a day, and continue for weeks. And at the end of my show, I would roll back my sleeve and invite the performers to dine." The man raised his chrome hooks in the air.

"I read that in Mexico, the Church supported flea art," I said. "Nuns made and sold miniature models of the stations of the cross fashioned out of flea corpses and scrap materials. The fleas kept them from having to carve human figures."

"I had a flea," he said in a quiet voice. "I kept it as a pet. It was the only one I let suck the palm of my hand. I fastened it to a chain of gold no longer than your finger. I attached a perfectly-shaped coach of gold to the chain for the flea to pull."

I thought I'd seen everything. But the way he talked about this pet flea and the perfect gold coach got me to thinking. "Yes," I said, my voice rising, "do you think you could tell me about it again?"

He stared at me. "No," he said, cautiously. "It's hard on me to remember."

I tried to think of a proper response. "I understand," I said, finally.

The man rubbed one of his metal claws against the skin under his chin. "Wait a minute," he said. "Get me something to write with."

He picked up one of the plain white lampshades. I placed a pen in his left claw. It was a felt tip pen that I had forgotten to return to the clerk when I wrote a check at the Winn Dixie grocery store.

He drew the whole flea circus on the shade, the wedding, the tightrope walker, and a flea ballet. He drew scenes we hadn't even talked about. Finally he drew what I knew had to be the flea on the golden chain, for it rested on the palm of a hand. The hand was perfect.

From time to time I tried to explain to people why I bought the lampshade. After a while, I moved the lamp next to my bed and shut the bedroom door.

SAVED
BY MR. F. SCOTT FITZGERALD

It was George who first told me about the nudist woman.

"There's no modesty left," he said, as he picked me up after work at the bookstore. And he was right. Even in the bookstore, a job I liked because of its slow pace and few customers, women were opening their blouses and suckling their babies right in front of the Motherhood shelf. George called them walking chuck wagons. It was enough to keep me from dozing.

The nudist woman's apartment was just a few doors down from mine. We pulled up in front of it in George's pickup truck. It was a little, foreign truck, the kind that's now being made in the USA. At the time, George couldn't afford the full-size American version. He couldn't even afford to put a radio in it. This was one of the reasons he had become so observant. "See," he said, pointing, "she's got her curtains pulled all the way back."

I looked at the house and, sure enough, there was a woman sitting there, in the downstairs apartment, as silent as a fish in a tank. Through George's binoculars, you could even make out that she was naked from the waist up, sitting at a table, eating creamed corn straight out of an open can. "George," I said, "this woman has just moved into this house. It's been vacant for a month. She probably hasn't even had time to put up her window dressings."

"That doesn't explain her chest," he said.

"It's hot. Men go topless all summer long."

"Yeah," he said, but I could tell he was thinking. He took his binoculars back, and took another long look. "You've got to meet her for me. Tell her you're from the Welcome Wagon or something."

This was how it always started. George would see a woman. Get me to meet her. Then we would introduce him into the picture in a real natural way. He said it made them more open to him, more receptive. But it never worked out too well.

The last woman, he saw in the bookstore. She was in the Psychology section, thumbing through a book on schizophrenia. I was just about to tell her that the bookstore wasn't a library when George motioned me to meet her. I tried to think of something nice to say. "My mamma forever told me as a child that it's OK to be schizophrenic as long as both your hearts are in the right place."

She looked up and smiled a sort of funny smile. Turned out she wasn't nutty at all. She just enjoyed reading books about people who were ill. Not just books about mental stuff, but any disease. The bookshelf at her house was filled with books on everything from Alzheimer's to zoophilia.

Her name was Jackie, and the initial part of George's first date with her went fine. They drove around in his truck, and she smoked a pack of Virginia Slims cigarettes. She had this fancy Zippo lighter that had a clear body that held the lighter fluid. Suspended in the flammable fluid was a pair of miniature dice. Every time she lit a smoke, she would shake the lighter and call out the number. "Seven," she'd say, or "Four," and she'd always follow the number by saying, "that's my favorite number." Then she talked about her classes over at the Auburn University extension college. She was in general studies, but she was thinking about changing her major to nursing. The word *nurse* was always a green light for George. It meant a woman *knew* something about anatomy and other things.

Then she told him how her brother had been run over in the street in front of her house and how when her mother had seen his body she had screamed that she had wished it had been Jackie instead. George didn't know how to respond to that, so he pulled the truck over to the side of the road, real slow and easy. Then he put his arm around her and tried to touch her breasts.

She took a felt-tip pen off of the dash of his car. It was a pen he had borrowed from me at the bookstore. She started writing on his jeans. It was too dark for George to read what she was writing. I would have wondered whether the ink would come out in the wash, but love makes you stand for funny things.

After he dropped her off, he came by my house and stood under my yellow bug-away porch light trying to read his pants. When I heard him whistle long and hard, I opened the door and let him in. "Look at this! Just look at this!" he was shouting, and pointing at his pants.

He explained to me how he came by the marks. He was forever telling me what happened to him. Right there emblazoned on his inner thigh in a pretty script was the word *copulation,* as plain as day. Above it, as if floating on a cloud, was the caricature of an intertwined couple that looked a lot like George and Jackie.

He wasted no time in driving around to the open service stations, searching for an appropriate condom. There was something about all those books on disease that had prompted him, but, after all, he said, a nurse would expect him to be professional. The service station choices were limited. The French Tickler, with its octopus-like extensions, seemed too personal for a couple's first time, and yet, to George, the plain old rubber Trojan just didn't seem sophisticated enough. Those were the days before glow-in-the-dark prophylactics or condoms with miniature batteries and moving parts. He felt optimistic enough to purchase one of each.

He entered her apartment filled with expectation. She had some piano music playing in the other room. He came right out and asked her if he could sleep over. At that moment, her daughter came out of the back room. She was waving her hands and screaming. The girl had the longest fingers George had ever seen. They were twice as long as normal fingers. She was waving them in front of her like she was warming them over a fire.

Jackie hugged the girl to her and told her to hush. She took her back in the other room and the music started again.

When Jackie came out, George was just sitting on the couch. "She's my daughter Jenny. She's an *idiot savant*, just like her dad."

"Her dad?"

"Met him over at the institution. I was doing volunteer work. He liked to play the piano. He was good with his hands. He and Jenny's one of the reasons my mom wished I was dead when she saw my brother was the one she backed over in the drive."

George didn't know it had been her own mother who had run over her brother. He wanted to say something about it. He also wanted to ask about Jenny's fingers, but just then he felt some other hands going to work up and down his leg. He cleared his throat. "Well, ah, what did your dad say?"

"I only heard my dad speak about once a year. He'd grab his shotgun on New Year's Day, walk out into the front yard, and fire a shot into the ground. Then he'd say the words 'Bad earth, bad earth,' over and over, like the lawn was a truant child."

"Things didn't go too right for him?"

"The earth finally won," she said. "Mom gave me the gun to keep.

116

It's the only thing I have left of my father's. I keep it right by my bed, just in case."

Somehow the hand on George's leg felt a bit rough.

"You want to turn in now?" she asked. "Jenny normally stays in the bed with me, but she'll be asleep in a few minutes. You just wait a little bit out here on the couch."

Only the fact that she had recently installed one of those double-deadbolt locks on her door, the kind that takes a key on the inside to open it, kept George from slipping out into the night. He sat on the couch and decided to pull the old I'm-Sound-Asleep ruse. He stretched back on the couch, full-length, and commenced to lightly snoring. As facts often follow fiction, he was soon really asleep.

When he woke up, he imagined he was still dreaming. He saw Jenny, the little girl, waving her long fingers in front of her like she was warming them over a fire. Only this time he could really see the fire. Then he saw it was his pant's leg. She had set his pant's leg on fire with Jackie's fancy lighter, and his flaming pants were setting the couch on fire. "Two," Jenny said, "that's my favorite number."

When the fire truck came, George drove off without saying his good-byes. His leg wasn't burned. Only the hairs had been singed, and his good jeans ruined. He could see Jackie in his rear view mirror, still talking with a fireman about all the different types of burn cases that he had seen.

George got me to introduce him to a nice Christian girl after that. She was a member of my Baptist church family. But that relationship didn't last too long because of his record collection. He would get a special price at The Record Shop on albums that didn't sell too well. One Sunday he made the mistake of playing a new Yoko Ono album on his stereo, just as his Christian girlfriend came walking up his drive.

She told me that she didn't have to listen twice to know that the moans of ecstacy were coming from an Oriental woman he had in his house with him.

I pondered for several days the question of how I could meet the nudist woman for George. Finally, the bookstore answered for me. She entered the store fully clothed, but I could still tell it was her. She went back and started looking around in the fiction section. I walked over and asked her something I rarely said, "Can I help you?"

"I'm looking for a book by Mr. Fitzgerald."

"What?"

"You know, that author that lived in Montgomery."

I was taken a bit aback. The store's bestseller had consistently been the *Bible*, followed a close second by *Gone With the Wind*. In fact, in front of the Baptist church there was a sign that proclaimed "Montgomery, Alabama, is #1 in Bible reading!"

"You know, Zelda's husband."

"F. Scott Fitzgerald."

"Yes, he's the one. I live in his house. Well, just the downstairs part. It's apartments, now."

This was my chance. I didn't know that Fitzgerald had lived down the street from me. I guess he had to have lived somewhere. "Oh, yes, I know your house very well. Yes, the Fitzgerald place."

"My landlord told me that it's the last house left standing in town that he and Zelda lived in. That's why he doesn't allow tenants who smoke."

After the Jackie incident, I knew that George would be glad to hear that the nudist woman didn't smoke. "Books by F. Scott Fitzgerald," I said, trying to remember what I had learned in the fresh-

118

man English course I took before dropping out of college, "ah, yes, Gatsby, *The Great Gatsby.*" My teacher was always going on about that book, something about some doctor's eyes and a green light. It was still the age of the great literary-symbol hunters.

"Gatsby?"

"Yes, he looks something like Robert Redford." Luckily I had seen the movie. "He's rich. He's got lots of shirts. That's how he attracts the girls. They like to see his shirts."

"Did he write that book in Montgomery?"

Now it's a shame that people expect folks who work in bookstores to know something about books. I didn't know where Fitzgerald had written the book. "The biscuit of it is that critics aren't too sure," I confided. "He was very secretive. Drank a lot, too." I was losing her interest. "But I have done my own study, and yes, yes, that's the book he wrote in your house." Her eyes opened wide.

"Do you have a copy of it?"

The plan came into focus. "No," I said, "it's a *classic* work of literature. It's very hard to come by in bookstores. But I'm sure I have a copy of it in my home library." I lied. Actually, the only reading material I was sure of having around the house was a *Bible* and a two-month old copy of *Playboy.* George had loaned it to me from his collection. He had every issue ever printed, cataloged and filed in their own special cabinet. "Why don't I drop a copy of it by your house on Saturday morning?"

"Can you make it Saturday night? Saturday's a busy day. I work at City Florist. I'm a funeral designer."

"A funeral designer?"

"You know, I make the flower arrangements for the funerals. Blankets of carnations to go on top of caskets. Broken wagon wheels cut out of styrofoam and covered in chrysanthemums."

"Now that must be an interesting job." I thought about my dull surroundings.

"It is, it is. Once a woman came in and wanted me to make an arrangement to look like a shotgun. I cut out the styrofoam to look just like one. I spray-painted the flowers brown for the stock and silver for the barrel. It was pretty."

"The deceased must have been a big hunting enthusiast."

"No, she told me he was a suicide."

"Oh." I didn't know what else to say. I wondered if she ever went to funerals, just to see how her work affected people, kind of like how a playwright might sit in back of a theater during a performance.

"I'd better be going. I'm gonna be late to work," she said, before I had time to ask.

George couldn't have been happier if I was making him a box of Kraft macaroni and cheese. George must have said more good things about Mr. Fitzgerald and his book than a whole room-full of college professors. When he had said his final "God bless *Gatsby* and Mr. F. Scott Fitzgerald," he turned to me and asked to see the book.

"I don't have a copy of it," I explained.

His face fell. "But your home library?"

I held up a copy of my *Bible* in my right hand and *Playboy* in my left. "This is the entire contents of my home library," I said.

George looked at the *Playboy* issue lovingly, the way a student looks at a test question he had actually studied for and could answer with ease.

"The bookstore?"

"Can't order it in time."

"The other bookstore?" There was a chain store at the new mall.

"It's a *literary classic.*"

George looked downcast, but George was always a thinker. He ran to my phone and called the public library, not that either of us had a borrower's card. He waited while the reference librarian checked the status of the book. When she came back on the phone, his whole body looked like it was sucked down into the ground all the way to China. He slammed the receiver into its black cradle.

"Out!" George hollered. "Out for two weeks. Why would someone check out a book that isn't even new?"

"It's OK," I said. "I'll just tell her I couldn't find it."

"Don't you understand? This isn't just a book. It's the first thing she's asked of us. It's . . . it's a *quest.*"

George always liked to use that word *quest.* He picked it up where he worked, at the King Arthur Burger Court. George had advanced in the last year to assistant manager, his uniform had the name Sir Lancelot emblazoned over his pocket, and the word *quest* was used repeatedly in his management training manual. He used to be a student at the Methodist College and Seminary in town, until he kind of snapped one day, dressed up in their basketball team mascot hawk outfit, and started preaching across Montgomery, saying the words to all who would listen, "Oh, Israel, that I could gather you up like a hen gathers her chicks . . . ." The hawk outfit was just old enough and in poor, sagging shape to give George the look of a giant mother hen.

He sat down on my one good chair, a La-Z-Boy. He pushed his weight back all the way and his feet shot up in the air. Somehow, the way he was sitting there, all sprawled out like a tire with no air, made that chair look like the world's saddest recliner.

Finally, he said the only words he could muster, "We have been betrayed by Mr. F. Scott Fitzgerald." It was a melancholy exclamation, born of mental exhaustion, and that's the way he sat for about an hour.

I had only seen him like this one time before. We had gone up to the Lake Jordan Dam, to do some fishing. We waited for hours with our cane poles in the water, watching the red and white bobbers floating up and down with the wind. The fish were not biting. We were just drowning one worm after another.

A man walked up to us and asked us how we were doing. I said I hadn't caught a thing, but George's imagination did not live on a small budget.

He started to tell the man how he had been catching catfish all day, so many, and so quick, that he had to just keep letting them go. He was just about to go into great detail about how one was bigger than me, since I'm about a foot shorter than George, when the man asked to see George's fishing license. He was a game warden. He wrote George a ticket for fishing without a license, but he let me go, since I hadn't caught anything.

After the man left, George just sat on the bank, looking the same way he did about this *Gatsby* business. Finally, I had to just load all of our stuff back in the car. George followed along, quiet like, and didn't say another word on the drive back to Montgomery.

I barely had spoken the words, "I wish I'd finished my freshman English course and not sold my books back to the college," when George shot up out of the recliner like Jonah from the whale's belly.

"College!" he shouted.

"But, George, I went to school out of state."

"Not yours, mine. Professor Peter J. Dickinson at the seminary.

He has his own collector's library." George grabbed me by the arm like a fishing pole on a sunny Sunday afternoon. He deposited me in the passenger's side of his truck and screeched down the street towards the Methodist College and Seminary.

The Methodist College and Seminary parking lot was a busy place to be on a Friday night, all because of the Red Lady. Years before, a rich woman attended the college. She was obsessed with her money and the color red. Her room was decorated in red. Everything she wore was red. She didn't make friends easily. When she received a letter from her father saying that they had run out of money, she hung herself in one of the top-floor rooms. It is said that if you watch long enough after midnight, you can still see her unearthly, crimson image in one of the rooms on the top floor of the building. It was the traditional Southern date suicide story. For some reason, women in the South expected you to tell them a horrifying story before you attempted to unsnap their bras. This was one of the reasons for the popularity of the parking lot in front of the main building of the Methodist College and Seminary. It's also the reason for the proliferation of Southern authors.

The building was laid out simply. The first floor was administrative offices and the chapel. The second floor was classrooms and faculty offices. The third floor was the men's floor. And the fourth floor was the women's.

We got out of the truck and walked past a row of cars with fogged windows.

When we arrived at the office door of Dr. Peter J. Dickinson, there were signs of life coming from it. There were more than signs of life, there was genuine liveliness, from the smell of burning hemp coming out from under the door to the giggles of a person considerably younger than Dr. Peter J. Dickinson.

George knocked on the door. There were the sounds of furniture and clothes being rearranged. Then there was chanting. "Ommmmm."

Eventually, the soft words of the good doctor called to us, "Enter in peace."

The room was heavy with the medicinal smell of Lysol air freshener. Dr. Peter J. Dickinson was sitting cross-legged on the floor, next to a beautiful, raven-haired coed, the kind of young woman whose clothes must be grateful to so perfectly contour her body. Things seemed a bit blurry to me in the room. I felt funny. They both had their hands raised in the air, as if they were trying to attract signals from some Far Eastern radio station. "We can continue our meditation session tomorrow, Mary Lee. The incense seems a bit strong, in here, but . . ." the professor was saying, until he looked up and saw it was just us and not some official group of administrators and parents.

"Dr. Dickinson?" George said.

The mixed emotions of relief and irritation fought to gain precedence over the professor's facial features. "What? Who? Young men, you have interrupted a very important religious experience." He paused and looked right at George.

Maybe it was the incense that was doing the talking for Dr. Peter J. Dickinson, but he started laughing. Not just an ordinary laugh, but the kind you laugh when you finally get grape jelly at McDonald's for breakfast, instead of mixed fruit, or you find real paper towels in the bathroom, instead of one of those hot air blowers. It was the laughter of small miracles.

"Chicken Boy!" he howled.

George's face went red.

124

"You're Chicken Boy!" The professor turned to Mary Lee. "This is Chicken Boy!"

Then Mary Lee started laughing. "Why," she exclaimed, "you're more famous than the Red Lady. All my teachers talk about you in their classes."

"Everyone wanted to know what happened to you," Dr. Peter J. Dickinson, said, "after the incident and all."

They were alluding to the chicken-suit preaching incident. George had to go up to the hospital in Birmingham for a while.

"He's in hamburger," I blurted out.

"I didn't expect him to be at Kentucky Fried Chicken."

"The quest," George threw in. I could tell he did not want me to go any further into his current occupation.

"Quest?" the professor asked.

"We are in dire need of a copy of *The Great Gatsby.*"

Dr. Peter J. Dickinson's eyes were bright. He tasted a story bigger than a King Arthur Burger Court Royal Burger, the kind of story professors dream of finding to one day top those told by their colleagues in faculty mailrooms and lounges.

"As it so happens, I do have a rare, first edition collection of American authors." He pointed to a fancy, glass-fronted bookcase. "These books are priceless," he said, more for the benefit of Mary Lee.

"We only need to borrow your copy of *The Great Gatsby.*"

"Fitzgerald's masterpiece of preposterous love and the superannuation of traditional American belief . . ." Again, Dr. Peter J. Dickinson waxed a bit for Mary Lee's sake.

"Right," George said. "About the book, can we . . . "

"I'm sorry, but it's far too valuable to loan out. It's inscribed by the author, you know."

George looked through the glass at the book the way a hungry dog looks through a butcher's window. The professor unlocked the case and took the book out. It was sealed in plastic, so you couldn't open it. He handed it to George to look at. I had only seen a moment like it one time before. It was an exhibition of trained German shepherds. These big dogs were made to stand very rigid and still, while their trainers placed dog treats on top of their noses. Their look of desperation and anger reminded me of the look in George's eyes.

"Note the dust jacket," the professor said, no longer for Mary Lee's benefit, but more in the celebration of knowledge itself. "It was painted months before the book was finished." The cover had a pair of these big brooding eyes. "The artist thought he was painting Daisy's eyes, but when Fitzgerald saw it, he wrote them into the book as the eyes of Dr. T. J. Eckleburg. Hemingway thought it was the ugliest thing he'd ever seen."

I wanted to ask about the shirts. I thought I remembered Robert Redford throwing an armful of beautiful shirts up in the air and Mia Farrow crying into the glorious pile because it made her so sad that she had never seen such beautiful shirts before. I wondered whether that had been in the book or just the movie. I thought maybe I'd better read the book, it being a classic and all, and that way the next time someone came into the store asking about it I'd know something to say, but George's hand on my sleeve interrupted my reverie.

In the background the professor was still talking, something about colors and symbols and the American Dream. But George was pulling me from the office. Pulling me from the thing he most desired.

George's heart was breaking into about a million pieces and falling into the wasteland of accumulated King Arthur Burger Court soda cups and burger wrappers on the floorboard of his truck. George believed in his quest, but that Fitzgerald book kept receding before him. To have it in his hands and then . . . no matter. George was always one to say, "Tomorrow, I will run faster, I will stretch out my arms farther . . . ."

"Boats against a current," George said, as we slowly drove back to my house.

I wanted to say the word *persevere*, but it wasn't a word that came naturally to me. It was a word I had seen in the title of several self-help books at the bookstore. When I finally managed to speak, I said the word "preserves."

"With hot biscuits," George said. I guess I couldn't have said anything better. Food was the small consolation for life. "Or sausage gravy." George smiled.

Right at that moment it became clear. We were just a few doors down from my house, and there was the sign. The nudist woman's lights were on. No, it wasn't her lights. She was sitting in a chair in front of a television set. The curtains were still not up. Her naked body was bathed in the blue light coming from her TV. The National Endowment for the Arts couldn't have funded a more artistic vision.

"She is an angel on Earth," George said. Then he hit the gas pedal, and I knew where we were heading.

If there was one thinking spot in Montgomery for a love-sick man, it was Hank Williams' grave. It was the place that the local police always visited to drink beer and celebrate a big drug bust. It was the place George and I always went to when his heart was falling apart like a dropped jigsaw puzzle.

The songwriter's grave was in the oldest cemetery in town, just behind a row of Confederate graves. This was actually his second grave. His first plot was too small for a fitting monument, so they dug up a couple of French pilots who had died in a crash at Maxwell Air Force Base and moved Hank to their spot.

The monument was a respectful marble slab, and on top of it was a stone cowboy hat. The titles to some of his songs were etched into the slab. George always read them out loud like a litany, "Your Cheatin' Heart . . . I Can't Help It if I'm Still in Love with You . . . ." At the top of it, it read, "Praise the Lord, I Saw the Light." Then there were clouds with giant sunbeams breaking through them. Beside Hank's grave, there were marble benches for the weary to sit on and think about life and death.

After George recited the song titles, he would start to sing. As the night wore on he really did begin to sound more and more like Hank himself, wailing away. George would sit on the slab and sing, and I would fix the drinks.

I dropped a whole aspirin each into two bottles of Coca-cola, although I preferred to pour a package of salted peanuts into mine, but it was a Southern form of dope used since the miraculous invention of the dark elixir in Atlanta.

George finished his bottle in one long gulp, and started singing about a whippoorwill who felt too sad to sing. I nursed mine along a bit. Hank Williams' stony white monument shimmered in the night. All was still, giving the place a kind of serene beauty. The scene was communicating something to us. Something about how you needed to live life. Thinking about Hank's body reclining on the ground below me made me want to spend as much time as I possibly could standing up.

George stood up, too. He touched the red artificial roses that filled the two marble vases beside the grave. It was one of those swift moments of decision that would lead him irrevocably towards ruin or salvation.

It was only after we had gotten back to the car that I realized that the *Gatsby* business wasn't over. Now I'm a bit gentle-witted, but I'm also one of the few honest people I have ever known. But what George proposed would end all of that. I would have to become wise and less than honest. George wanted me to provide a diversion. "That bookcase, it's right in front of the window. All of those necking fools out front, waiting for the Red Lady, would see us up there."

"We will need your red dress," George said. I knew what he meant. It was really Scarlett's red dress in *Gone With the Wind.* Rhett made her wear the dress to Melanie's party, after a group of old biddies put the word out about how she was seen hugging Ashley.

George had entered a Southern Costume Contest at the National Guard Armory. George wanted to go as Rhett Butler, but his girlfriend at the time had walked out just as they were getting dressed for the event. She had found a pair of women's underpants in his laundry basket. George tried to explain that he had dropped off his laundry at his mother's, that there must have been a mix-up in the dryer, which was true, but George was never too lucky in his explanations to women. George pleaded with her not to desert him until after the contest. He had spent a lot of money on the costumes, but she used Rhett's own words against him. "Frankly, my dear," she said, "I don't give a damn."

I will not tell you anymore about that night just now. Suffice it to say that I would be recreating the role of Scarlett for the second time in my life.

They say that practice makes perfect, but my second performance as Scarlett was tinged by a certain world-weary quality. I guess I had gained a bit of weight since I had last suited up. In the dark, inside the

Methodist College and Seminary building, George helped me pull up the zipper. I had to almost completely hold my breath in order not to bust out of the gown.

George's part of the mission was to climb through the window over Professor Peter J. Dickinson's door and steal the book. He had a tiny penlight to use to help select the correct volume.

In the dark, I climbed the stairs to the fourth floor. If the dress hadn't been so tight, someone could have heard me wheezing. George had told me that at the center of the floor was a laundry and ironing room that had windows that looked out towards the front. He gave me a candle to light and carry in my hand, while I pranced back and forth, up and down, in front of the glass, pretending to be the ghostly Red Lady.

When I entered the room, I could barely see. The windows were open, so I walked towards them. I lit the candle and started my distraction. Then I heard a voice.

"Professor? Peter? Is that you?"

I stood as still as death. My heart pounded in my chest. I gasped for a breath. The restrictions of the tight dress made the quick intake of air impossible. I did what any other normal, corseted, Southern Belle might do. I fainted.

When I came to, I was in the arms of Mary Lee. She recognized me as the friend of Chicken Boy from our visit to Dr. Peter J. Dickinson's office. She thought it was the sweetest thing that I had dressed up like a woman to sneak all the way onto the fourth floor to see her. She also said she found the idea of making love to a man dressed up like Scarlett O'Hara kind of exciting.

My mother told me that as a baby, she read *GWTW*, as she calls it, to me in my crib, but I could not remember anything from the book to prepare me for the rest of that night.

George waited for me outside, but when I didn't show up, he decided I could find my own way back. The quest could not wait.

He drove over to the nudist woman's house.

She answered the door wearing a Japanese kimono. George explained how I had asked him to deliver the book. He was sorry he was so late, but he had seen her light on. He said it was his own copy. It was a signed first edition.

She invited him in. He sat in the same chair where he had so often seen her sit. She unwrapped the plastic cover that the professor kept around all of his collectable books. She touched the jacket cover gently.

She opened the book to the first page, but something was wrong. Something had changed in her expression. The title on the first page read *The Illustrated Kama Sutra,* even though the cover had proclaimed it to be *The Great Gatsby*, and, under the title, there was a picture of two people intertwined in a way that would seem humanly impossible.

George wanted to explain that somehow the cover must have been on the wrong book, but the woman started screaming something about him being a pervert. Then she started hitting him with the book. George's hands flew out in front of him. His hands were shaking. He told me later that his fingers looked real long, waving out in front of him, defending against the potency of literature.

George went running out into the dark night, his arms outstretched in front of him. He jumped in his truck and drove all the way through town, back to Hank's grave.

He started singing again. A forsaken cry went up among the graves. Then, in the moonlight, he saw her. She was beautiful. She was the first woman he had ever met without my help. She was drawn to his song. She was a stripper down in one of those New Orleans clubs. She said she always did it to Mr. Williams' music. She was wearing her tiny work clothes. She was on her two-week vacation, and she said that she just wanted what was left of Hank to see her act, and, by George's account, it was enough to raise the dead.

George helped her get a job at a local Dairy Queen. Later that month George was promoted to full-time night manager at King Arthur Burger Court and got to wear a real crown. Over his uniform pocket, they embroidered King Arthur. You might say that George and his new girlfriend became the king and queen of Alabama fast food.

I didn't see George but a few times in the months that followed, but it didn't matter because I always knew that there were people like him left in the world, people of honor who would follow their quest to the end, steadfast and ceaseless. About the others? For understandable reasons, Professor Peter J. Dickinson never mentioned the break-in or the loss to his extensive pornography collection, and the nudist woman bought some unbelievably thick curtains.

Me, I'm actually reading that book, *The Great Gatsby,* and those shirts are really in there. I'm also thinking about going back to college. Mary Lee has convinced me that there's a real benefit to education. So you see, in a way, we were all saved by Mr. F. Scott Fitzgerald.

If you enjoyed this work, you will likely enjoy our other publications:

Fiction

Tom Abrams, *A Bad Piece of Luck,* novel, ISBN 0-942979-23-0, $9.95

W.C. Bamberger, *A Jealousy for Aesop,* stories, ISBN 0-930501-13-6, $9.95

James E. Colquitt, editor, *Alabama Bound: Contemporary Stories*, ISBN 0-942979-26-5, $13.95

L. A. Heberlein. Sixteen Reasons Why I Killed Richard M. Nixon, novel, ISBN 0--942979-30-3, $9.95

Maureen McCafferty, *Let Go the Glass Voice,* novel, ISBN 0-942979-28-1, $9.95 (Due Spring of 1997)

Natalie L.M. Petesch, *Wild with All Regret,* stories, ISBN 0-930501-07-1, $10.95

Louis Phillips, *Hot Corner: Baseball Stories and Humor*, ISBN 0-942979-36-2, $11.95

B. K. Smith, *Sideshows,* stories, ISBN 0-942979-16-8, $12.95

William F. Van Wert, *Don Quickshot,* novel in verse, ISBN 0-942979-32-X, $9.95

Allen Woodman, *Saved by Mr. F. Scott Fitzgerald,* stories, ISBN 0-942979-41-9, $9.95

Allen Woodman, *The Shoebox of Desire,* stories, (all contained in this book you hold), ISBN 0-930501-11-X, $ 8.95

Poetry

Cory Brown, *A Warm Trend,* ISBN 0-930501-19-5, $8.95
Michael J. Bugeja, *Flight from Valhalla*, ISBN 0-942979-12-5, $9.95
Cynthia Chinelly, *Coralroot*, ISBN 0-942979-01-X, $5.00 (chapbook)
Stephen Corey, *The Last Magician,* ISBN 0-930501-17-9, $9.95
Stephen Corey, *Synchronized Swimming*, ISBN 0-942979-14-1, $9.95
B.H. Fairchild, *The Arrival of the Future,* ISBN 0-930501-01-8, $8.95
Charles Ghigna, *Speaking in Tongues*, ISBN 0-942979-20-6, $11.95
Ralph Hammond, editor, *Alabama Poets*, ISBN 0-942979-07-9, $12.95
R.T. Smith. *The Cardinal Heart*, ISBN 0-942979-09-5, $8.95
R.T. Smith, *Hunter-Gatherer*, ISBN 0-942979-34-6, $9.95
Eugene Walter, *Lizard Fever*, ISBN 0-942979-18-4, $12.95 (illustrated by author)
Michael Waters, *The Barn in the Air*, ISBN 0-942979-00-1, $5.00

If you order directly from us, please add two dollars for postage.

Livingston Press
Station 22
The University of West Alabama
Livingston, AL 35470

Allen Woodman was born and raised in Alabama. He was edu-
cated at Huntingdon College and Florida State University. Besides
publishing scores of stories in magazines and anthologies, Woodman
is the author of a comic novella entitled *All-You-Can-Eat, Alabama*
and two children's picture books. He now lives in Flagstaff, Arizona,
where he directs the Creative Writing Program at Northern Arizona
University.